Summer
LIFEGUARDS

ELIZABETH DOYLE CAREY

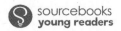

sourcebooks
young readers

For Alex

Published by Sourcebooks Young Readers, an imprint of Sourcebooks Kids
P.O. Box 4410, Naperville, Illinois 60567-4410
(630) 961-3900
sourcebookskids.com

Library of Congress Cataloging-in-Publication Data
Names: Carey, Elizabeth Doyle, author.
Title: Summer lifeguards / Elizabeth Doyle Carey.
Description: Naperville, Illinois : Sourcebooks Young Readers, 2021. |
    Series: Summer lifeguards ; 1 | Audience: Ages 8 | Audience: Grades 4-6
    | Summary: "Follow Jenna, Piper,
    Selena, and Ziggy in this exciting new series starter about the power of
    friendship, community, and being grateful for what you have"-- Provided
    by publisher.
Identifiers: LCCN 2020049579 (print) | LCCN 2020049580 (ebook)
Subjects: CYAC: Summer--Fiction. | Friendship--Fiction. |
    Lifeguards--Fiction.
Classification: LCC PZ7.C2123 Sum 2021 (print) | LCC PZ7.C2123 (ebook) |
    DDC [Fic]--dc23
LC record available at https://lccn.loc.gov/2020049579
LC ebook record available at https://lccn.loc.gov/2020049580

Source of Production: Versa Press, East Peoria, Illinois, United States
Date of Production: June 2021
Run Number: 5022630

Printed and bound in the United States of America.
VP 10 9 8 7 6 5 4 3

CHAPTER 1

Jenna

TUESDAY

I initially heard about the storm as I packed my backpack at my locker at the end of the first day of school. I was distracted, thinking about an assignment my friends and I had all just received in English class. Our new teacher wanted us to write a paper about what matters to us in life. (*Duh! Swim team!*) It had to be two pages long and was due next week. No problem. My paper about the swim team would practically write itself.

But something else caught my attention: a sixth grader named Allie was saying, "My mom said it might be a Category Five by the time it hits us."

"What are you doing to get ready for it?" asked her friend, who was also in the grade below me.

"I don't know. Last time we got hit by a big one, our chimney got blown off the house and it scattered bricks all over our neighbor's yard. And my grandma's basement got filled with five feet of water. She didn't have power for two weeks after."

"My sister's a lifeguard and she said the last one we had caused the biggest waves she's ever seen here, *and* it created riptides that lasted for three whole weeks!" said Allie.

I slammed my locker shut and turned. "Is there a nor'easter coming?" I asked, hefting my backpack over one shoulder. I was bringing home all of my textbooks so I could do some prereading and map out some chapter study guides while we still had a light homework load. I pulled my blond braid out from under the shoulder strap of my backpack and looked down at Allie. I'm always taller than everyone, especially sixth graders.

Allie shook her head. "Hurricane. Shaping up to be a biggie too. Hitting the Caribbean tomorrow, then the southern U.S. coast, working its way up the Eastern Seaboard."

"Wow!" My eyes grew wide. With a fisherman for a dad and farmers on my mom's side, I was pretty tied to the weather, and even though I hadn't heard anything about *this* storm yet, I knew enough to take hurricanes seriously. We'd had some doozies over the years. "When's it due here?" I asked.

"Saturday," said Allie.

What?

"Saturday! But it can't come Saturday! That doesn't work at all!" I sputtered. A huge storm would interfere with the regional swim meet I was supposed to attend up on the North Shore on Saturday. A storm could make me late, or even keep some competitors home, competitors I needed to face in order to climb the state rankings. All my training over the summer, for what?

Allie looked at me strangely. "I don't think we have a choice."

I took a deep breath. "Right. Right." I shook my head and took out my phone to look at the weather report as I walked away. I was sure Allie and her friend were exchanging glances behind my back, but I didn't care. I needed the facts.

Sure enough, Hurricane Trina was gathering strength in the Caribbean and heading to make landfall in the Bahamas tonight. I offered up a silent prayer for the people there, that the hurricane would spend all its power somewhere out on the open sea and never make landfall, and then just melt into a rainy day by the time it reached us. That was what usually happened up here, and *that* wouldn't make me miss my meet. That, I could stand.

I took a minute to visualize the storm, then correct the image for a win. This is one of the mindfulness things that our swim coach taught us to do when we're nervous about something. In my own mind, I call it a vaccination because it feels like it protects me: I imagine the worst possible outcome of a situation, then correct it to be the best possible outcome.

I closed my eyes and pictured dark clouds moving into Westham. I pictured heavy rain and strong winds bending trees, maybe snapping some limbs, scattering leaves everywhere. I pictured the ocean whipped up into a white froth, people walking on the beach with their hair blowing back and their clothing stretched tight against them from the wind. I pictured my dad telling me the meet was canceled. Then, I corrected it all for the win. I pictured Saturday as a bright sunny day, maybe a little windy, with some afternoon showers. I pictured my hand slapping the touchpad of the pool in Salem, time after time, for a win. That's all. Perfect. I opened my eyes and smiled in relief. I was using these new mindfulness techniques pretty much every day, and I liked them.

Outside school, I stowed my phone, snapped on my helmet, and hopped on my bike to ride to swim team practice. It was a beautiful, sunny, late-summer day, and there wasn't a cloud in the sky. There was no *way* a hurricane was about to hit here. I was sure it would veer away from the coast. I was sure I'd make my meet on Saturday. There was nothing to worry about. After all the practice and training I'd done all summer, there was no way I'd miss that meet.

Especially if my teammate and direct competitor, Franny Barnes, was going.

As I rode to the YMCA, I reviewed the summer in my mind. It had been hard work, but I was *pretty* sure it had been worth it. And it hadn't been *all* work and no play. If I looked back, I knew I'd done a *few* fun things with my besties, Selena, Piper, and Ziggy. Like, I think we went to mini-golf up the Cape once (or was that last summer?), and I knew my dad had taken us out on his boat one time—though we didn't make it all the way to Nantucket for nachos as planned. I knew Piper had slept over twice and I'd slept at Selena's once. Oh! And I'd gone to a Chatham Anglers Cape Cod Baseball League game with my cousins for three innings after a swim meet once. (My town, Westham, is too small to have its own team.) That was fun! I had also made some money working mornings at my mom's family's farm stand whenever possible. Four hundred twenty-seven dollars to be exact. That was time well spent.

But most importantly, I shaved seven seconds off my 50-yard butterfly.

Swim team does not stop for summer. Dryland training, swim practice, and traveling to meets doesn't slow down just because school's out. In fact, it ramps up. With all the extra free time, our coach—and the coaches who organize meets all over New England (and probably the world)—look at the summer as an empty ocean of time to be filled. This summer, Coach Randall added three practices and two training sessions a week, plus a new weekly mindfulness program designed to help us relax and focus. All this plus twelve meets, many of them off-Cape, made for a busy summer, most of it spent underwater.

Some kids might think this was boring, but not me. I love to compete. Any training that might give me an edge is something I want to try. I liked the mindfulness stuff for this reason, and I liked the yoga we tried a few times too. I logged it all in my swim journal, along with my times, which went steadily down over the twelve weeks of summer training.

It was too bad I'd had to miss my friend Kelly's birthday party again in July. It's always on the same weekend as the regional meet. This was a bad party to miss, though, because my friends had talked about it for the rest of the summer. Every time I saw them, they were all, "And then Kelly had make-your-own sundaes," and "Then we did levitation at two in the morning," and they'd laugh. But team sports are about sacrifice. No pain, no gain. I'm all in.

That's why I can't wait for the Mid–New England Regional coming up this weekend. It will be the proving ground for all my hard work this summer, and I am dying to see how I do, especially against mainland girls I only face twice a year. I plan to win. Correction: I plan to beat Franny Barnes. That will be winning enough for me for now.

Because the meet's a couple of hours from here, my dad will drive me up super early Saturday morning—like at 4:45 a.m.—and we'll spend the whole day there. I'll pack healthy snacks and lunches for us, my yoga mat, and my headphones so I can listen to my meditation app between heats. My dad listens to audiobooks in between races—or he sometimes talks to the other parents, but they're super-competitive about their kids, so it's not a friendly group.

School only started today, and summer already seems like a distant blip on my radar screen, even though yesterday was Labor Day. In some ways, it's easier for me when school starts up again. There's less temptation to do fun stuff rather than practice, and everyone's on a schedule. For example, my friends are planning a day of fun this weekend, also known as "Let's Pretend It's Not Fall Yet" Day, which I will be missing. To start, Selena wants us all to do beauty treatments at her house on Saturday morning, because she's going to be the star of the school play and she wants to look her best. I'll be missing that.

Then, Ziggy suggested we all go to Vinny's Pizza on the dock afterward to get vegetarian slices for lunch. After that, Piper wanted us all to go to Lookout Beach and scope cute guys. (I don't know where she's gotten this new obsession with boys, by the way. It's weird. All the boys we know are nerdy or immature, and I can't imagine thinking *any* of them are cute. She talks about cute lifeguards sometimes too, but they're, like, old compared to us. Maybe sixteen or seventeen, even.) Anyway, I won't be back in time for that either.

But none of that matters, because I will be long gone by the time they get their first face masks on at Selena's. I'll have competed in three events by the time they're picking green peppers off their pizza, and I'll be waiting for my final race by the time they're packing up their towels to leave the beach. It's okay, though, because I'll be getting my name out there, posting times for all to see, and furthering my goal of one day reaching the Olympics or the U.S. Naval Academy, or both. That's all that matters.

Right?

Coach Randall was doing her pre-practice spiel.

"Girls, I've been getting word of a storm approaching. It might hit here Saturday, making it tough to get to the meet."

There were groans across all the lanes of the pool. I slapped at the water to release some frustration. Maybe my dad would agree to get us a motel room in Salem, and we could go up the night before? Unlikely, due to the expense, but I made a mental note to ask him later.

"We just need to be prepared," said our coach. "I'll be updating the website daily, and I'll send out an email to all of you and your parents Friday night to confirm our plans. In the meantime, we're going to taper the workouts for the next few days. We'll work smarter than ever—not harder, because I don't want to exhaust you—to win that regional. I want each of you to win as individuals, and I want us to collectively win as a team. This means supporting your teammates, even if you're competing against them. Got it?" she let her eyes roam across all of us.

I stole a glance at Franny Barnes next to me. She looked poised and composed, her dozens of tiny dark braids beaded with pool water, her large brown eyes focused calmly on Coach Randall. Why did she never show any emotion? It annoyed me that she was always so calm. It made me feel like I was hysterical all the time.

Franny must've felt my eyes on her. She turned placidly in my direction, looking right through me, then back at Coach Randall, as if she hadn't even seen me. It made me so angry whenever she did that! There is nothing worse than having a rival who doesn't even acknowledge your existence! It's so humiliating. Like, she's so much better than I am that she doesn't even notice me? If she went to my school, it would drive me wild to be ignored by her all the time!

"One more lap, girls, then you can hit the showers."

We all got into position at the head of our lanes.

"Swimmers, take your marks..."

I took a split second to glance at Franny next to me. Her chin was dipped low, her eyes drilled on the far end of the pool: total focus. And it was at that split second that the coach blew the whistle. And it was that split second by which Franny beat me.

CHAPTER 2

Selena

TUESDAY NIGHT

Ay, Díos, I hate being back at school! Even though my summer wasn't amazing, it was better than having to do homework or sit rigidly in school for hours a day. Also, after the report card I got in June, my papí says I have to have at least a B average by midterm, or he is canceling all my social media accounts, which I only just set up! The pressure is on. I feel the drudgery piling up, like in *Working*

Girl, that old classic movie with Dakota Johnson's mom—all work and no play.

Well, except for *the* play.

They announced today at the all-school meeting that the fall play auditions begin this week. I nearly leapt out of my seat when I heard what it was: *Little Women*! It's a great book (well, I've actually only seen the movie, with Saoirse Ronan and Timothée Chalamet), and I'm going to try out to be Meg, the oldest and prettiest of all the sisters (Emma Watson, in the movie). I couldn't wait to get home and start primping ASAP.

Meg is the best role, because getting it is basically a recognition of beauty. Sure, there aren't a ton of lines to learn. I think it's more about posture and presentation and looking great, but I can do that. I just need to imagine what's going on inside Meg's head, and then I can be her. I can sit on stage and silently think her pretty thoughts and look pretty and let everyone fall in love with me! That's my plan.

I hope they won't mind having an Ecuadorean Meg. It shouldn't matter, though, right? My hair is long and chestnut-colored and wavy, just like Meg's. My skin is clear and smooth, my eyes are big and brown, and people tell me all the time that my face is heart-shaped, and I look like Tori Vega. I *think* that means I am pretty enough for the part. Maybe I need just a little tweaking, though.

There's a meeting tomorrow to hand out the script to anyone who wants to audition, and then we have the first auditions on Thursday, with a callback on Friday for kids who made the first cut. I'm praying to be called back for Friday, and to get the part, of course. Jenna texted me earlier that there's a storm coming this weekend. Maybe it will be all cozy after school on Friday for the callback.

The only time I like being at school is after hours, actually. It's fun to be in that strict place but with less rules— like, I could do cartwheels down the empty halls and sing anywhere, and no one would say, "Indoor voice, please, Miss Diaz," or "Settle down, now, Selena. Time to focus!"

That might even be part of why I like doing school plays: getting to be at school when things are chill.

Classes today were the usual blah blah: "This is your textbook," and "Please make a note of my email address so you can contact me to schedule extra tutoring." Yawn. As *if* I'd ever contact a teacher in order to make plans to see them more than I already do.

With school starting up, I'm going to have to fit a lot into my after-school time. Skin and hair treatments and improvements, vocal exercises, wardrobe assessments (I like to plan out "costumes" for everything, since outfit choice is a big part of a character), and social media. I'm building my brand so that when I finally launch as a star, I will already have a following. I read about all this in an article on the *People* magazine website that talked about Kylie Jenner and Rihanna and Taylor Swift and Serena and Venus Williams and how they've all built such amazing brands. It's work, work, work, but I'm not afraid of hard work.

As long as it's not schoolwork, that is.

"Selena! You'd better not be online again! If I come up there and find you..." My mamí's voice was threatening, and I didn't need to even hear what my punishment would be to know that she meant it. I quietly closed my laptop and turned back to my homework. I had a chemistry worksheet to do, and I had to brainstorm for a paper for English about what matters most to me. (Being a big, beautiful movie star, claro!) Both assignments would take a while, so I went with the chemistry first, since my parents love math and science, and I am terrible at both.

My parents are obsessed with success. Ever since we moved here from Ecuador when I was little, it's been about the work. My papí runs his own landscaping company, and my mamí is studying to be a certified public accountant, but in the meantime, they are the live-in housekeeper and caretaker at a big fancy estate here in Westham on Cape Cod, Massachusetts. The family who owns it—the

Frankels—live in London and only come for two weeks each summer, so the rest of the time, we have the run of it all.

My mamí, papí, my older brother Hugo, and I live in a small guest cottage at the foot of the property near the driveway entrance, but the lawn swoops up far, far away to the big house up on the dunes, passing the tennis court, gardens, pool and pool house, and in-ground trampoline on the way. Our house is cute, but pretty small for the four of us, so I like to spread out on the Frankel property. I often post pics on social media from the porch of the big house or with a tennis racket on the court. No one needs to know it's not really my house. If I look rich and fancy, people will assume I am rich and fancy. That's good enough for me.

Meanwhile, back to my science homework... Chemistry makes no sense to me tonight, and it was only the first day. I sighed and very quietly opened my laptop. I searched "Best Homemade Beauty Remedies" and watched the results roll in. I wanted to do something to enhance the glow of my skin for the play auditions, something that would make a major impact. I scrolled through the listings intently, so intently that I didn't even notice my mamí until she swiped the computer out from under my hand and tucked it under her arm and left the room.

I sighed in aggravation and turned back to the chemistry. She'd check my work before she'd give me the computer back, so I had to dig in. Yuck.

It was eight o'clock by the time I'd finished all my homework and eaten dinner. If it were summer, I'd be settling in for a movie about now, but there was no time for that kind of research on school nights. I still had all my beauty work to do. After my mamí made me check my homework to find the two errors she'd spotted, I got my computer back.

"Finally!" I muttered.

"Selena!" warned my mamí. She doesn't allow freshness

(or any of the -nesses: laziness, brattiness, selfishness, the list is end*less*, haha!).

Upstairs, I went back to my online search and reviewed the many complicated but highly successful beauty remedies I could make and do at home. There were ways to remove your mustache (I looked in the mirror: Do I have a mustache? Díos mio, I'd never thought of it before!), tricks to brighten the whites of your eyes or your teeth, things you can do with mayonnaise to make your hair shiny, scrubs for skin brightness. All sorts of ideas. I found two that I liked—the tooth whitener and the brightness scrub—and printed out the recipes, then I went to collect the ingredients.

The tooth treatment was easy. It called for baking soda from the kitchen and hydrogen peroxide from the medicine cabinet. I mixed them together (It exploded for some reason—who even knows why these things happen?) and used it and found that my teeth were, actually, a little brighter. That was cool. There was a nice lifeguard at

Lookout Beach this summer who had the most amazing even white teeth. They made him look like a movie star, and I wanted to look like that too.

The face scrub—well, actually, I picked a body scrub recipe, because I figured it was stronger and that would be better—called for ground sea salt and olive oil. We only had coarse sea salt, but I figured that would be okay. Maybe it would even work better. My face would glow so beautifully on that stage that even from the back row, no one would be able to take their eyes off me.

I mixed it together into a rough paste, then I closed my eyes and patted it all over my face. It smelled kind of gross, but what can you expect. I began to rub it in, and I have to admit, it hurt. That surely meant it was working. I rubbed harder because *beauty is suffering*. I once heard that somewhere.

I'd forgotten to check how long to do this for, but after a while it was really burning so I tried to wash it off. Only I couldn't get all the oil off, so I fumbled around with my eyes closed until I found a towel and mopped my face off with it. I looked in the mirror, and my face was bright red and felt like it was burning. I needed something to cool it off...quickly. I cast my eyes around the bathroom and spied my brother Hugo's Sea Breeze. He uses it on his face to prevent acne, and it says *Cooling* right on the front of the bottle. I soaked a cotton ball in the liquid and rubbed it all over my face. I almost screamed it burned so bad, but that meant it was really working, for sure.

Looking at my face in the mirror now, I winced. It was bright red, and there seemed to be tiny scratches all over it, like a miniature cat had clawed at me. Well, those would disappear overnight, and I'd be glowing at tomorrow's play meeting, for sure.

I smiled at myself in the mirror to admire my white teeth, but I winced as my cheeks moved and the smile turned into a grimace. So, I switched off the bathroom light and headed back to my room. But something caught my eye, and I turned back to look out the window. There was a light on upstairs at the Frankels'. That was weird. I'd have to tell my mom she left it on when she was cleaning up there today. Just not right now, because I needed to update all my social media!

CHAPTER 3

Piper

WEDNESDAY

At lunch today, the talk was all about Selena. She'd missed school today and no one knew why. Who misses the second day of school?

"Piper, have you heard anything from her today? I've left two voicemails, and she hasn't even texted me a word in reply," said Jenna, taking a bite of the turkey wrap her mom had packed for her lunch. Her big brown eyes looked worried as she chewed.

I had leftover spaghetti from the dinner I'd made myself last night. It was okay, but I sometimes thought lunch would taste better if someone else made it for me. Like, it would be nice to be pleasantly surprised by the contents of my lunch bag, just once.

"Isn't the first meeting for the school play today?" I asked. Inwardly I shuddered—I couldn't *imagine* being up on a stage with all those eyes on me, but Selena loved it, thrived on it, even. I guess if I were as pretty as she was, instead of the hulking blond giant that I am, I might like the attention too.

Jenna nodded, inspecting the chips and brownie her mom had packed. "Yep. No way would Selena miss that if she could help it."

"Anything on social media?" I asked, twirling the cold noodles on my fork.

"Nothing," said Jenna, her eyebrows knit in concern.

Ziggy shook her black curls and dipped her fork into her grain bowl. "She's probably *really* sick if she's not snacking."

I laughed. "Snapping! It's called *Snapchat*, Ziggy, not Snackchat. How many times do we have to tell you?"

Ziggy isn't allowed to have a phone or computer—her mom thinks they just make you want to buy stuff and that they give you brain tumors—so she relies on us and on the computers at the library to keep her up to speed. Sometimes I think she hams up her cluelessness a little, just to make us laugh. The no-phone thing doesn't really seem to bother her; it all fits in with her family's hippie lifestyle, anyway.

I have to have a phone, since it's just me and my grandma, Bett, on our farm—the Janssen Family Farm. She sometimes gets stuck with a horse giving birth or having colic, and she can't pick me up from a friend's. Or she'll text me from the barn and ask me to get dinner going or throw the wet laundry in the dryer. Also, I need the phone to talk to my mom a few times a week. She never knows when she might have the time to call me from Pennsylvania, so I have to be ready.

"I hope no one's dead," said Jenna grimly.

"Gosh, Jenna! I hadn't thought of that!" My throat tightened in fear. The Diazes don't miss school unless... Well, Selena's actually never missed school, that I can think of. Her brother Hugo chopped the top of his pinkie finger off one night at work, and his mom made him come to school the next day with it sewn back on and all wrapped up. "Should we call her house?" I asked.

Jenna shrugged. "I already did. No answer."

"Her parents are at work, I'm sure. I'll stop by on my way home. It's only two more hours until we get out."

"It's not exactly on the way," said Jenna.

I shrugged casually. "No prob."

The truth was, I'd been dying to get over to Selena's neighborhood—where all the fancy summer-house people live—for days now, and this was the perfect excuse. See, I'd fallen in love this summer—not with a person, but with a house. Only, the people who owned it were summer people, and now they were gone, so the house was closed for the winter, and my heart was broken.

The Petries were from Beacon Hill in Boston, and they were so wealthy, the parents didn't even work. Campbell Petrie, the youngest daughter, and I met in June, when she arrived with her horse for us to board. We clicked so fast that she invited me to sleep over on the very first day we met. The Petries' house was, to me, the prettiest, biggest, and best house in Westham. Gray-shingled with white shutters, it had twelve bedrooms, a massive wraparound porch that overlooked the ocean, and an attic family room with squashy couches and a big screen TV with Netflix and video games, and even a pinball machine. It wasn't just that the house was so fancy—it was that everything was in perfect condition, and there were so many people to take care of things. They had housekeepers and a house-man and a cook and a gardener. The Petries didn't have to lift a finger. I'd seen a little bit of this lifestyle from being over at Selena's—the Frankel house is shockingly impressive—but I'd never seen it from the rich person's side before, only the workers' side.

The Petries had three kids, and the one I matched up with was Campbell, the youngest. Her older brother and sister were mostly away this summer, but her parents had lots of guests, and there was always the staff bustling around. It was all so unlike the quiet, empty, tiny, plain house where Bett and I lived alone.

Campbell was cool, but her house was *amazing*. I loved being over there so much that I sometimes even imagined I *was* a Petrie. When Campbell and her family and her horse, Jagger, left at the end of the summer, I cried. I hugged her goodbye and sobbed into her shoulder, but what I was really crying about was her house and the great snacks and meals they always had and how someone was always home, the lights were always blazing, everything was clean, and you didn't have to do it yourself. It was heaven.

Now, real life felt flat. It had only been a week since the Petries had left, but it seemed like forever, like it had all been a dream. I'd never been friends with summer people before and hanging around them felt so different—it was almost like it had ruined me for real life.

I had figured that when school started, I'd get caught up in homework and field hockey practice and canning vegetables with Bett, and, of course, barn work. But all day yesterday as the teachers introduced our new classes, I doodled drawings of the Petries' house in my notebook. Our English teacher assigned us a paper called "What Matters," right as I was drawing the Petries' attic. The attic has these cute little dormer windows with window seats in them, and there was a widow's walk on the top, which you could get to through a trap door in the roof. Campbell and I would sometimes go up there and pretend we were the brave wives of sea captains in the olden days, waiting for our husbands to come back from their sea voyages.

"What matters," my teacher was saying. "What matters to you?"

A widow's walk matters, I whispered to myself. *A third*

floor matters. Someone to cook for you matters, I said to myself, almost giggling out loud.

Back at today's lunch, Jenna was speaking again. "Okay," she agreed. "Call me as soon as you get to the Diazes', okay? And tell me if they need anything. I can text my mom from swim practice to let her know."

Local families here stick together. Farmers and fishermen like Jenna's family, horse and farm people like my family, people who work the land, who work hard, who are out here full-time in the bone-chill of winter—we need each other to get by. For a long time, the Central American families who'd started immigrating here in the 1990s were not considered local, even though they lived here all winter and the kids went to school with us. But now, enough years had passed that they were accepted and had become part of the community—going to church, volunteering as EMTs and firefighters, joining the PTA, and organizing school bake sales—so they were considered local too. Now, if one of those families suffered, everyone stepped in, just like they would with the families that had been here forever. Casseroles would appear, rides would be offered, logistics would be handled, and care and help would be given. That's how you survived in a place like this, where the winters are cold and lean, and the summers are flat-out hard work. You stuck together.

"Hellooo? Leeny? Mrs. Diaz?" I knocked gently on the screen door.

The door was unlocked, so I peeked in. The kitchen was neat—it didn't appear that anyone had fled here in a hurry, which was a good sign. Outside, Mr. Diaz's shiny black pickup truck was gone, to work for sure, but Mrs. Diaz's baby-blue Crosstrek was neatly parked. *She must be up at the big house, cleaning*, I thought.

I pulled open the door. "Selena?" I called in a louder voice.

I heard a thump from upstairs. I cocked my head. "Selena?" I called in a louder voice.

"Mmmhhh!" I heard. It was definitely Selena, but what was wrong with her? Why couldn't she talk?

"Leens?" I called. As I made my way to the stairs, I allowed myself an admiring glance around. Mrs. Diaz kept their house as neat as a pin: The couch cushions were always perfectly fluffed, and the remotes and books on the coffee table lined up like soldiers. It always smelled good—a little like baking and a little like sage—and it made me want to flop down on the cool, crisp sofa and wait for dinner to be ready while I watched TV.

At the top of the stairs, I turned right to Selena's room. Her door was closed so I knocked and gently opened it. Inside, the shades were drawn, and it was dim, but Selena was there, sitting in her bed.

"Selena?"

She reached out and snapped on the light and my jaw dropped.

"Selena! What happened?" I raced to her bedside, staring at her face. It was bright red and swollen, with a million needlelike scratches all over it, like she'd been attacked by a tribe of vicious seamstresses. It looked awful and super painful.

She opened her mouth a crack. "Can't talk," she mumbled.

My hand flew to my mouth in shock. "Why?"

Selena gestured impatiently toward her desk. "Paper," she muttered.

"You have paper cuts?" I asked in confusion.

"Get paper. Pen," she muttered, barely moving her lips.

Quickly, I stood and grabbed a notebook and pen off her desk and handed them to her. She scribbled on the page and handed the notebook back to me.

Did homemade face scrub. Total fail. Agony! she had written.

I was perplexed. "Wait. You did this to yourself?"

She nodded and sighed heavily, rolling her dark eyes dramatically, Selena-style.

I clapped my hand over my mouth, then I removed it. "Why?"

She grabbed back the paper and pen. Beauty treatment gone wrong, she wrote.

"Oh Selena!" I shook my head, but I had to kind of laugh.

She looked at me for a second, then she started to laugh too, only it hurt.

"Ow, ow, ow!" she moaned.

"I'm so sorry, Leeny. How awful. What can I get you? What can I bring you? Here. Write!" I thrust the paper back at her. She scribbled for longer this time.

Nothing, thanks. Miss my phone. Mamí took it bc she is furious at me. She gave me cold compresses, but there was something important up at the Frankel house, so she's at work. What is homework? OMG, I cannot believe I missed the play meeting today. I am so pathetic. This hurts so much.

I looked glumly at Selena's face. "It will probably be better by tomorrow, right? I mean, maybe they'll let you audition anyway."

She grabbed the paper back from me and wrote,

furiously this time. CANNOT TRY OUT NOW! LOOK LIKE A FREAK! PLUS DO NOT HAVE SCRIPT!

I read it and sighed. Now was probably not the time to fight her on this. "Let's wait and see how it looks tomorrow. I'm happy to go to the drama teacher with you to explain."

Two fat tears rolled out of Selena's eyes, and she cried as the salty water hit the open wounds on her cheeks. "Ow, ow, ow!"

I grabbed a tissue and pushed it at her. "Here! Quick!"

She blotted her eyes and shooed me away. "Go!" she said through rigid lips.

"Are you sure?" I felt horrible for her.

She nodded morosely.

"Oh, Selena. I'm so sorry. Are you sure there isn't anything you need?"

She shook her head sadly.

"See you tomorrow?" I said.

She nodded and I gave her a quick hug, avoiding her face, and I left.

Outside, I stopped to text Jenna that Selena was okay. *Beauty treatment gone wrong. Face a mess but otherwise fine*, I typed. Jenna must've been waiting for my text because she replied immediately.

Phew, she wrote, with a relieved-face emoji.

I put my phone away and took a deep breath. *Go home, Piper*, I told myself. *Go home, now.*

But my bike had a mind of its own, and, like a pony coming back from a trail ride and smelling its oats in the barn, it took off where it wanted to go—toward the Petrie house that I missed so much.

A few blocks later, I turned left into their driveway and sailed down its long swoop then pumped hard up the hill to where the house perched on a dune. My stomach flipped in happiness at seeing it again. *See?* The house seemed to be telling me. *The people are gone, but I'm still here!* A smile bloomed on my face as I set my bike by the steps to the back door and climbed to reach the end of the wraparound porch.

It was breezy along here, and the floorboards creaked as I turned the corner to the center of the porch and my long blond hair lifted off the back of my neck. All the outdoor furniture had been put away, and the windows were boarded with shutters, though one was banging in the wind somewhere. The house looked desolate, abandoned, sad, and my heart sank. Without the Petries in it, the house was flat, unanimated, lonely. I felt worse here now than before. At least when I imagined it, the house was brimming with life, filled with people and noise and light. The end-of-summer reality was different.

I sat down heavily on the edge of the porch, where the long flight of wooden stairs ran down to the water, and I looked out over the waves rolling in. Jenna said there's a hurricane that's supposed to come this weekend, but the ocean today looks as calm and normal as it did all summer. Maybe the hurricane thing is a rumor.

Living in vacation land—also known as Cape Cod, Massachusetts—you have to "Make hay while the sun shines." That's what Bett always says. She means you have to work really hard while the vacationers are here so you can make all the money you possibly can before they go home for the winter. Summers are frantic when you own the fanciest horse stables on the Lower Cape, as we do. From Memorial Day to Labor Day, we're packed with visiting horses, demanding clients, pony camps, small jumping shows, day trippers looking to do trail riding on the beach, and more. It's wild!

So normally, I love the end of summer. All the hubbub at the barn dies down, summer clients take their horses home, and we close two of the barns for the winter. That means less stalls to muck out, less horses to curry and feed and exercise, fewer chores around the house, and a little more of Bett's attention. In town, the lines at the ice cream parlor and the movie theater go away, the beaches empty out, and we get the place back to ourselves.

But this year, it just feels lonely and flat. I miss the Petries. I miss pretending to be a summer person, rich and cared for. It was so relaxing being here with them—like I didn't have a care in the world. It was fun.

Suddenly, I heard a car door thunk. My heart lifted. Could it be them? But no, of course not. School was in session. They were long gone, back to Beacon Hill and their private schools.

A heavy tread approached on the porch. Someone was coming, and I was frozen in place, trespassing.

CHAPTER 4

Ziggy

WEDNESDAY

"Please, Ziggy, can't you see? It's just capitalism run amok!"

My mom was on a roll, railing against the government, the media, and our money-hungry society. It was hard to stop her when she got like this. I think she kind of thrived on the energy it gave her. I just had to sit and listen for a minute or two, then I could casually escape to my room—my cocoon—without her really minding. I took a deep, centering breath just like my yogi taught me, and I tried to stay present for her rant.

Today's topic? Hurricanes. Specifically, hurricanes and the shopping that they encourage as well as the panic and disarray the government creates around them.

She went on. "Listen, they just use these weather events as economy boosts. I see it year after year! Okay, maybe down south it's a real thing, but here in Cape Cod— they freak everyone out, people rush to the stores and buy out all the food and supplies, then they go home with their flashlights powered by poisonous batteries and their generators full of fossil fuels and their full larders, then the government turns off the power, the food rots, and the storm passes by with just a few raindrops. Nothing! It's all a trick."

"Hmm," I said, not wanting to commit one way or the other. Agreeing with her could fan the flames of her anger, while disagreeing could also enrage her further. Not knowing what I really thought about this topic, it was best for me to sit in near silence. I lifted my long black curls and twisted them into a bun on top of my head, then I folded myself into the lotus position on my stool. It sounds hard, but when you're as small as I am, you can accomplish surprising things.

My mom banged around in the cupboards getting her yogurt-making supplies ready. "And—aha! I just thought of *this!*—have you ever noticed how these hurricanes are always *right* at the end of the summer? Right when all the greedy local stores take stock of what they didn't sell all summer and realize how much inventory they need to move? Then the so-called hurricanes come, people rush in and buy up everything and—ta-da!—inventory sold, shopkeepers happy. And you think the government's not behind that? Yeah, right! The sales taxes line all their pockets!"

I didn't have an opinion about the government's role in hurricane spending one way or the other, but I wasn't about to say so. I just nibbled on my blueberry spelt muffin and watched the clock. In about another forty-five seconds, I could legitimately say I had homework and duck away.

"And the radio news is talking about evacuation! Ha! We aren't anywhere near the ocean, and they're talking about moving all the people in Westham out of our houses. I tell you, this is just how the process of eminent domain begins. They get us out of our houses for an emergency, then they say the houses are in unsafe locations or why would we have evacuated, then the next thing you know, the houses have all been seized by the government and a road is being built through here. Like Joni Mitchell sang, *They paved paradise, put up a parking lot!*"

"Mmm-mm," I mumbled, not wanting to commit. I practiced more deep yoga breathing to center myself and not get caught up in the angry aura my mom was creating.

She banged the ceramic pot on the stove top and snapped the cheesecloth out to unfold it, then she flung open the door of our vintage fridge and withdrew a glass bottle of the milk from our neighbors' cows that we'd bartered our chicken eggs for. She clunked the bottle down heavily on the counter and sighed, then spun to face me with her hands on her hips.

"So that, my dear Ziggy Stardust, is why I have not made 'plans' for the hurricane." She was practically panting after her rant, and she blew a wisp of her dark bangs off her forehead.

I shrugged. "Okay, sounds good," I said, regretting that I ever asked. I slid off the barstool at the kitchen island top (which was a thick oak door my parents had salvaged from the freecycle area at the dump) then shook out my cloth napkin in the sink and set it aside for later use.

My mom looked at me as if assessing whether I agreed with her or if she still had more ranting to do to convince me. I avoided making eye contact; I just wanted to be alone for a little while and write in my journal and maybe meditate to center myself before starting my homework.

It was only the second day of school, but seventh grade

was already showing signs of toughness. Besides math, reading, and Spanish vocab flash card–making, I had a lab report due for chemistry on Monday, and I needed to see if I had all the data I'd need for it, or I'd have to get it at school tomorrow. I don't have a computer at home (my mom thinks they're used by the government and big business to spy on us), and I don't own a cell phone (ditto, plus my mom says they cause brain tumors), so I can't easily reach kids if I am missing homework or any info I need. I also have to write a paper for English on what matters. Hmm. *Everything* matters? Garbage, pollution, carbon footprint, wasting water, animal extinction—every little thing matters. Oh, and having a mom who's not so ridiculous. That matters too.

"Ziggy?" said my mom, as I slipped my rucksack over my shoulder and headed up the stairs to my room. I stopped and looked down at her.

"Stay vigilant," she said. "Don't ever sell out to the man."

"I won't!" I said lightly, and I scurried away to my room.

When I was little, I always thought "the man" was a real person, that there was a big man somewhere who was scary and giant, like Paul Bunyan. I used to be terrified that he'd come and find us. But it turns out "the man" is an expression people use to mean the government or people in power. My mom and my dad always say how they didn't like working for "the man" in New York City, so they moved us up here to the Cape full time when I was a baby. They also talk about their protests and civic actions as "sticking it to the man." I think that means getting back at the government.

My room is my happy place. I have my futon on the floor, and I have Indian tapestries and batik scarves and all sorts of floaty fabrics draped from the ceiling to create a cave-like feeling around it. I have little twinkly fairy lights strung up and a thick rag rug that my mom made for me, and all around are little pieces of nature I've collected: shells, dried flowers, rocks, crystals, jars of sand from beaches I love. I dove onto my bed, snuggled under the quilts, turned on my AM radio (freecycled!), and reached out for my little bottle of amber oil, which I dabbed on my wrists for aromatherapy. Then I did deep breathing until I started to feel calm and centered again. *Aaaah!*

I stretched and grabbed my books and pulled them into my cozy cocoon to start my homework. Only, reviewing my notes brought me back to school today and all the kids talking about the hurricane. Everyone was preparing in some way.

Jenna's family was harvesting everything they could to reduce spoilage on the farm. They were frantically canning vegetables and making jams and freezing things—anything they could do to make some money from their crops before the hurricane laid waste to them. Meanwhile, Jenna was praying the hurricane would miss us so she could get to her swim meet.

Selena's parents were securing everything at the

Frankel estate—draining the pool so it didn't overflow, putting away all the outdoor furniture, closing all the shutters and boarding up windows that didn't have them, and lopping dried branches off trees so they didn't become projectiles in the wind. Also, they had a surprise visitor to look after, which added a wrinkle to everything.

Piper's grandma was transporting any horse she could off the Cape. It wasn't only because their farm was near the ocean and vulnerable to flooding. It was also because horses can get spooked from the storm and accidentally injure themselves in their stalls.

All of my friends and their parents and grandparents and brothers, sisters, cousins, whoever, were busy, busy getting ready for the storm.

And my family (in other words, my *parents*) were the only ones who *weren't*. I wondered who was wrong and who was right. Logic told me that if everyone else was getting ready for something, I probably should be, also. But if my mom had given me one lesson my whole life, it was this:

Don't do things just because everyone else is. So now I wasn't sure what to think or do!

I chewed on the end of my pen as I thought. The storm was set to arrive late Friday. At a bare minimum, we were supposed to get a ton of rain. We live right next to a pond, and the chances were good that it would overflow, which could flood the house.

Our house uses solar energy, so we are off the grid, as my mom says. If the town's power goes out, we'll still have power, which is cool. I only worry about our house flooding and all of my parents' fruits and veggies dying in our small field, and what about our chickens? Gary the rooster and all his "ladies"? Also, what about the animals around town? And the old people and poor people who I volunteer with in my knitting group and at the food pantry? Who will look after them?

This was starting to stress me out a little. I took more deep breaths and focused on my homework for a while, nailing the math and my grammar worksheet in one big push. I needed to be done quickly because I had my knitting club tonight, filled with grandmas (not mine, other people's). I decided to see what *they* thought about the storm, since I didn't have any grandparents, aunts, uncles, or cousins to check my parents' opinions against. Though my knitting friends' opinions often clashed, I could usually get good advice out of listening to them all and then looking for a theme or two to follow. I'd see what tonight's themes were.

Okay, there was only one theme tonight, and it was "Get the heck out of your house!"

Yep, all the grandmas in my knitting club (six of them, to be exact), said that hurricanes were things you just don't play around with, and we should plan to be evacuated from our house.

"Honey, get your chickens over to Iaconos Farm and

let them board them for you. They're on high ground, and Bob's weathered a storm or two." That was Mrs. Fitzgerald, queen of the heel turn for socks.

Mrs. Moretti, who knits a killer afghan blanket, said, "Get everything off the floor of your house—loft it or stack it. Prepare for at least three feet of water. If there's less, you've been lucky. Then go!"

And Mrs. O'Neil, the angora sweater master of the Lower Cape: "Get to the shelter early to make sure your sleeping spots aren't next to the bathrooms. Pee-yew!"

"But we're not leaving," I protested. "We have solar energy and my mom refuses to buy any supplies and my parents both say that the government will seize our house if we evacuate."

I saw some of the grandmas exchanging glances, but I wasn't sure what that meant. Were they keeping something from me?

Finally, Mrs. Moretti said, "Ziggy honey, you've got to go. Even if you go on your own. Be safe. Come to one of us, even. We'd all love to have you and your parents! Just don't try to ride out the storm at home with the three of you alone."

This set all the knitting ladies chattering about who had the most space to offer us and why each of them should get us over anyone else. I love my pretend grannies—I wish I had a real one of my own, but my grandparents all died long ago—so I just fill in with my knitting club grannies and the volunteering we do together. It would be nice to have some extra family arms to hug me and family ears to listen to me, especially when my parents are being kooky, like now. Jenna and Piper are super-close to their grandmas (Piper *lives* with hers!), and even Selena speaks to both of her *abuelas* on the phone every Sunday, and she's going down to Ecuador for Christmas this year to see them.

When knitting club drew to an end at nine, I hugged all the grannies goodbye. I could see my dad outside, waiting for me in the Prius—that's our electric car. No need to fill it up with fossil fuel pre-hurricane! We could just plug it right in to our solar cell and power it up. Maybe my mom was right. It was clear outside, and I could see tons of stars. Maybe this whole hurricane thing *was* being overexaggerated by the news and the town.

"Hi, sweetheart!" said my dad as I hopped in.

"Hey, Pops." I pulled the door shut.

Inside, I heard squawking, and I turned around.

"Ladies! Gary!" In the back of the car were all of our chickens, free-range! "What's up with this?"

My dad put the car in drive and pulled away from the curb. "We're taking them over to Iaconos Farm for a weekend getaway, a couple of days early. A spa retreat!" he grinned at me in the dim light of the dashboard.

I grinned back. "The hurricane?"

He nodded.

"Good thinking," I said. "All my knitting friends are worried about us—and the chickens. They had suggested the same thing."

"They want us to stay in the barn at the farm too?" joked my dad.

I rolled my eyes. "No, they all want us to stay with them. Or, at least to stay at the hurricane shelter, wherever that ends up being."

"Hmm," My dad's eyes were fixed on the road straight ahead.

"What does *hmm* mean?" I asked, giving him the side-eye.

"Your mother would like us to shelter in place."

"And what do *you* think?" I asked. My dad was usually calmer and, to be honest, a little more rational than my mom.

He sighed heavily. "I agree that it feels like the news media hype these things way up and the government is always crying wolf, then things turn out not so bad—at least around here. In Texas and Florida and Louisiana, it's always *worse* than they predicted. But here, I also feel like you never know, and it's better to be safe than sorry." He turned and grinned at me. "So, I'm just trying to play the odds of whether it's better to be in a huge fight with your mom or up to my knees in flood water on Friday night."

"Right. Hurricane Lisa might be just as bad as the real one." Lisa is my mom's name.

My dad laughed. "Exactly."

We chatted about school on the way to Iaconos Farm and then on the way home, and I went right to bed when we got back. I was kind of avoiding my mom, just not wanting to engage with her and get her rolling again. Luckily, she went to bed quickly too, and my dad tucked me in.

But right as I was falling asleep, the phone rang. Ten forty-five was late for a phone call! I propped myself up on my arm and strained my ears to listen. Our house was small, which made for easy eavesdropping access, but my dad's voice was low. I could just make out what he was saying: "We're fine. It's safe, I promise. Thank you for checking in. You don't need to do this. We're on our own now, you know that. We've made our decisions, and this is our life."

Who on earth could he be talking to?

"Harry?" called my mom sleepily from their room. "Who is it?"

His voice got quieter, and my ears were nearly popping off my head to hear. But he was wrapping up the call and hanging up now, calling out to my mother that it was nothing, someone from his town environmental committee just checking in.

But that was so weird, because right before he hung up, I could have sworn he said, "Bye, Mom."

CHAPTER 5

Jenna

THURSDAY

"Dad, what happened here?" I was aghast.

My dad's mouth formed a grim line as we looked at aisle after aisle of empty shelves. The supermarket where my mom had sent us to buy batteries had been totally wiped out, leaving empty shelves and freezers everywhere, and people were milling around with blank looks on their faces, like zombies.

"People panic before a hurricane," my dad said in a sober voice. "There's not much anyone can do to prevent storm damage, so they go wild buying things they think they might need. As for the food shopping, it might not be the worst idea. If the storm is terrible, deliveries won't get out here for a while, so people are stocking up in case we're cut off like that."

"But why buy so much food?" I asked my dad. "If the power goes out, no one's fridge or stove will even work."

He shrugged. "It just makes them feel like they're more in control. And people use coolers with ice to store the food and then just grill outdoors if the power's out for more than a day or two."

My eyes widened at the idea. "Has that ever happened before on Cape Cod?"

My dad nodded. "Back in 1991, Hurricane Bob. Roads closed, power lines down, utility poles blocking roads, flooding everywhere, one-hundred-twenty-mile-an-hour winds, boats washed up on shore, chunks of the dunes and beaches eroded and washed out to sea, no power off and on for two weeks. It was horrible. And I know back in 1938 was the worst hurricane in modern history. More than six hundred people died on the Cape."

A chill washed over me. "How?" I gulped.

My dad looked thoughtful. "Drownings, mostly. They didn't evacuate from the low-lying areas in time." He shook his head. "It's not gonna happen, so don't worry. We have lots more notice now, with the news and the Internet and storm modeling and stuff. That's how we end up with empty stores, though." He waved his hand around the supermarket. "Let's go."

At school today, Ziggy was telling us about how her mom was freaking out at the government and the media, saying they were exaggerating the storm for money-making purposes. Now, after seeing the empty shelves, I kind of had to agree with Mrs. Lisa a little. It seemed as if people had gone totally over the top with their shopping.

Thank goodness my family grows or catches most of

our own food. Between my mom's family farm, where they grow fruit and veggies and raise chickens, cows, and pigs, and their family farm stand, where they sell gourmet prepared food and baked goods, plus my dad's fishing boat, we'll never starve.

My dad had been driving by school today when I got out, so he picked me up and we threw my bike in the back of his pickup. I had an hour to kill until swim practice, and he had wanted to run the errand for my mom, then stop by the town dock to see how his friends were doing with getting their boats storm-ready.

Now, we passed by the gas station and I saw a long line of cars waiting to get into the pumps.

"What's up with that?" I asked, turning my head to look back at the cars sitting there.

My dad glanced at them in his rearview mirror. "Filling up their cars to evacuate. In Hurricane Bob back in 1991, there was an eleven-mile backup to get over the Sagamore Bridge and off the Cape. People sat for hours. Since then, a lot of folks bought generators to keep some power on if the town loses it. Some of those people may be filling up gas cans for their generators."

"Do we have a generator?" I asked.

He glanced at me and grinned, "Nah. Generators are for summer folks."

I looked at him carefully. "Are you scared?" I asked.

He turned and smiled at me briefly. "No, sweetheart. Everything's going to be fine. It probably won't even hit us in the end. A lotta the time these things swerve at the last minute. Sometimes it seems like the more prepared we are, the less likely we are to really get hit, you know?"

I was silent for a moment, and then I asked the main question that had been on my mind for the past two days. "Do you think we'll make it to the regional meet?"

My dad pressed his lips together. "I... I'd say don't get your hopes up."

My eyes welled with angry tears, and I quickly blotted them with my sleeve. I wasn't about to get caught boo-hooing about a swim competition, even if I *had* been training for it for months.

I gulped hard. "Uh...is there any way... I mean, do you think we could go up tomorrow and spend the night?"

My dad took his hand off the wheel and patted my knee. "Jenna, I am nearly positive that meet is going to be canceled. And if it's not, I just can't afford to go renting hotel rooms and also, I certainly can't leave your mom and the boys during a hurricane, assuming it does hit. What if we got stuck up there? What if things were really bad here and I wasn't here to help?" He shook his head. "I'm sorry."

I nodded and bit my lip. I'd known what he was going to say, of course. And I knew he was right. I was sure that if I couldn't go, Franny Barnes wouldn't be able to go either, and that made me feel a little better.

My dad's truck cruised slowly down the steep switchback that led to the town docks. He had dry-docked his fishing boat on Tuesday as soon as he'd heard the storm was coming. And it was a good thing too, because the dry-docking lift was so backed up now with requests, they wouldn't be able to get all the boats out of the water before the storm came.

"Hey Mark," said my dad to an old dude, apparently a friend of his, who was walking down the road next to our truck. With my dad's thick Massachusetts accent, it sounded like he called the guy "Mock."

The old guy turned and smiled at my dad. "Bowers, heard ya got ya boat out. Yer no dummy, chip off the old block!" said the old guy with a cackle that showed he had very few teeth. He pushed his Red Sox hat higher up his forehead and mopped his brow with a dirty green bandanna. "Hope the rain will cool us off a bit. Hot end of summer we're havin', ayuh?"

"Yuh," agreed my dad. The Massachusetts accent seems to be stronger when fishermen are talking to each other than anyone else around here.

"Heard they got Slater running the town storm prep," said Mark. ("Storm" sounded like "stahm" the way he said it.)

"Oh yeah?" My dad raised his eyebrows.

Mark nodded. "Pro'ly gonna evacuate us."

"Yuh," said my dad. "Slater will enjoy that."

This made Mark laugh like a hyena until he started coughing and waving us on. My dad raised a hand in good-bye, and we continued our crawl down to the dock.

"Who's Slater?" I asked.

My dad's eyes were busy scanning the dock now, taking in all the activity. "Guy I used to know." He shrugged.

I sensed there was more to the story. "Do you like him?"

My dad pulled into a parking spot and shut off the truck's loud, rattling diesel engine, leaving us in relative peace. "He's all right."

I sighed impatiently. I wasn't going to get any more from my dad on this topic. I looked at my phone. It was 3:15. "We've got twenty-five minutes before we've got to go," I told my dad. Franny Barnes was always, *always* in the pool warming up whenever I got to practice. No matter how early I tried to get there, she always beat me. It drove me up the wall. But not today! Today *I* would be the early one.

"Ay, cap'n," said my dad, saluting me.

We climbed out of the truck and went to see what was what.

The docks were in total chaos. People were racing around tying things down on the boat decks, removing sails from sailboats, adding anchors to moored boats out in the harbor, and dragging dinghies out of the water and into the storage warehouse. I saw people hanging old tires all around the sides of the boats at anchor in the slips around the dock and asked my dad what that was all about. He told me the tires were used like bumpers, to cushion the boats if the waves rolled in and tossed the boats around. This way they wouldn't get smashed against the dock or each other. Everywhere, there were people calling out to each other over the sounds of revving engines and the usual twin smells of boat fuel and fish guts. Trucks were coming and going and piles of supplies—ropes, old tires, anchors—grew and shrank.

My dad headed toward the harbormaster's office and I followed.

Inside, it was bustling chaos. Phones were ringing and the Weather Channel was playing loudly on the TV mounted on the wall. It smelled like burnt coffee and cigarettes in there, and it was full of men.

"Bowers!" a bunch of them called out as my dad came in. I felt a warm glow inside me, knowing how many friends my dad had here and around town in general. He greeted everyone and offered his help. As his friends began filling him in on their plans, the door opened, and an older man stepped in. He was not very tall, but he had broad shoulders and a strong look to him. His hair was steel gray and his eyes were ice blue, and his skin was tanned and wrinkly. The crowd quieted as he stepped farther into the room and consulted a clipboard he was holding. Then he began to speak, and his voice was loud and commanding. Everyone listened.

"I need six more heavy anchors, someone willing to tow a boat over to Mashpee, any more tires people can spare, and maybe we could get a food truck down here—even the Good Humor guy would be a start. Who can help me?"

People started chattering and volunteering, but my dad stood back and watched this guy with a cool look and his arms folded. I wondered why he wasn't jumping in, offering to help, like he normally would. As people received their assignments and piled out the door, the room cleared out. Soon it was just us, the harbormaster, and the clipboard guy.

His eyes met my dad's. "Bowers," he said, giving my dad a quick nod.

"Slater," said my dad, nodding back.

They looked at each other for an extra second, then Slater turned and left the building. I looked at my dad but from the look on his face, I knew better than to ask him about that guy right now. My dad turned to the harbormaster and they began a lively discussion about wind speeds and tide levels, and I drifted to the smudgy window and looked out. Slater, whoever he was, was running the show out there, and a bunch of high school kids I recognized had just shown up and joined him. He was giving them assignments, and as they nodded and turned to get started, I recognized a few of them. They were lifeguards from the town beach. They must've been storm volunteers. *Storm troopers*, I thought, making myself giggle. It was hard to take the whole storm thing seriously when the sky was blue, and the water remained calm and glassy. I stepped outside into the warm and muggy air, leaving my dad and the harbormaster inside, and I sat on a bench and watched the older kids swarm around the dock, helping people. They looked like a team: they'd all put on red T-shirts that said *Lifeguard* on the back, and people were greeting them with happiness and relief.

I saw one of the lifeguard guys take over for Mark, the old fishing dude, who was trying to hang a heavy tire off the side of his boat. Mark gratefully handed the rope to the lifeguard and stood back to watch the boy secure it.

On another boat, two lifeguard girls were lifting a sheet off the rigging of a sailboat, and farther down the dock, two lifeguard guys were rolling extra tires out to various boats in their slips. Seeing the kids swarming around in their red lifeguard shirts was really cool. I admired them.

A Coast Guard cutter chugged into the harbor and pulled right up to the empty spot in front of the harbormaster's shack. The Coasties cleated their ropes to secure the boat in place, and two of them—an Asian guy and a girl with a blond ponytail, both in crisp blue uniforms—jumped off the boat. Seeing them was, for me, like seeing celebrities. I was always in awe of people in the military—they were so brave and selfless and in great physical condition with incredible training. Their skills were almost like magic. I watched them cross the dock and enter the harbormaster's shack. I wondered what they were up to.

I glanced at my phone. It was just about time to leave. I leaned back and closed my eyes to visualize the storm passing us by. I took deep mindful breaths, picturing myself winning at the regional meet, over and over again, and then my eyes snapped open as my dad appeared, ready to go.

In the truck, I tried to get a read on his mood, but he seemed far away.

"Dad, what was the Coast Guard saying?" I asked.

He turned as if just noticing me. "They're going to evacuate the whole east side of town."

My eyes bulged. We didn't live on the east side of town, but Selena and Piper did. "When?"

"Tomorrow. They're putting Slater and his team of lifeguards in charge," he said, with a bitter twist to his lips.

I paused, trying to think of the right way to ask, but finally just said, "Dad, what's up with you and that Slater guy? Is he a bad dude?"

My dad sighed as he turned the car into the Y parking lot to drop me off. He pulled up outside the entrance and stopped the car, then turned to look at me. "Bud Slater runs the town lifeguard program, among other things. I'm not a huge fan of the guy. I think he's pretty full of himself. But we have bad blood that goes back a generation, from our dads. It's petty, probably, but I can't help it. He'll do a good job, though, and the lifeguards are great kids."

I wanted to ask more, but I was early enough that I had a chance to get into the pool before Franny Barnes today, so I opened the door of the truck and hopped out.

"Okay. Thanks, Dad. See you later!"

"Have fun, sweetheart," he said.

Inside, I changed as quickly as possible, stowed my stuff, and dashed into the pool room. Ten minutes early!

But Franny Barnes was already there.

CHAPTER 6

Selena

THURSDAY NIGHT

Well, my face was a mess yesterday. It was such a mess that my mamí let me miss school. It was such a mess that I couldn't go to the audition today, even though acting is my passion and I wanted the starring role in the play more than life itself. I looked too disgusting to have the audience fall in love with me. I was crushed.

Except that my passion for drama was being fed anyway: we found an intruder in the Frankel house!

Only it wasn't *really* an intruder. Here's what happened.

The night I did my face scrub—Tuesday—I noticed a light on up at the Frankel house as I was updating my social media. I didn't think much of it, but the next morning, which was yesterday, as I was wailing and begging to stay home from school with my ruined face, I needed to get my mamí off my case. So, I said something like, "Oh, and you think you're so perfect, but you left a light on upstairs at the big house yesterday!" or something. But my mamí knew that she hadn't. So, she hustled up there and was gone for a very long time, which is unusual at this time of year but was very pleasant for me in my current situation.

It turns out—drum roll, please—that one of the Frankel girls, Samantha, who is my age (twelve) ran away from this junior boarding school in western Massachusetts where her parents had enrolled her against her will. She just took some money from her school account and hopped on a bus to Hyannis. Then she took a taxi to the house and had ice cream from the freezer for dinner and watched

TV all night. My mamí found her there still asleep in her traveling clothes, and then there were a million telephone calls to Samantha's parents in England and to the school and back to her parents, and then my mamí was cooking for her and talking with her and whatever. She told me not to tell anyone, that this was a private matter and the Frankels especially wouldn't want the press getting a hold of this information. I vowed my silence, but inside I was a tiny bit envious that Samantha Frankel was newsworthy.

I barely know her, but I have to say I was impressed by her nerve at running away from school! Only now she's staying with us, which is, like, super awkward because we work for her and she's, like, super-rich and we're super humble. Last night, my mom moved my brother Hugo down to the pull-out sofa in the living room of our house (which Samantha technically owns) and gave Samantha his room. I felt bad for him, but he is a saint, so he loves doing stuff like that. I swear, I wouldn't be surprised if he turned out to be a priest, except that he *does* like pretty girls (like

Samantha, with her tawny skin, dark-lashed hazel eyes, and long tangle of black corkscrew curls). Hmm.

I didn't see Samantha before I left for school this morning (I was incognito in a scarf and baseball hat), but we watched some TV together after I did my homework last night, before dinner. At first, we sat there kind of awkwardly, watching *So You Think You Can Dance*. But when we both laughed at the same thing, Samantha started to talk.

"So, what happened to your face, love?" she asked, sounding like a grown-up.

"Oh!" I was a little taken aback by the *love*. "Um, I did a beauty treatment that was an epic fail." The latest contestant danced on in the background as my face flushed even redder in embarrassment.

Samantha's dark eyes crinkled when she smiled, and she swung her heavy black curls over her shoulder and peered carefully at my skin. "Aggressive scrubbing?" she asked.

I nodded and sighed, meeting her eyes. "Yep."

"What have you put on it since?" she asked.

"Um, cold water?"

Samantha tsked and said, "When my mum was growing up in Somalia, the grannies all used honey on cuts as a healing treatment." She studied my face again. "But you might be better off going with the real stuff. Do you have any antibiotic creams?"

"Um, not really? I don't think?"

Samantha nodded briskly. "My mum's got an amazing cream up at the house. She uses it after she gets her laser treatments, to speed healing. We can go up after dinner and get it."

"Okay!" I agreed.

So, after dinner, Samantha told my mamí she needed something from the house, and that I would accompany her, and we set out. It wasn't dark yet, and it was still warm and humid; it felt like we were going on a summery adventure. I'd never been around the Frankel house with Samantha; only with my mamí, who was so careful and took off her shoes when she entered and changed into slippers so as not to leave a trace of her presence; she always used the back stairs, and she was quiet and contained in her movements. It always made me so nervous to be in there with my mamí, and I was always annoyed at seeing her so subservient, because trust me, that is *not* her personality.

But tonight, Samantha banged open the front door, strode directly up the front stairs in her clogs, flipping on every light as she went, and chatting loudly while I trotted along behind her. We went right to her parents' bathroom, and she flung open the big medicine closet and began scanning the shelves.

"Aha!" she said, selecting a silver tube and brandishing it at me. "This will do the trick!"

I looked down at the tube and saw that it had a pharmacy label on it.

"It's prescription," I said.

"So?"

I looked more carefully at the label. "It was three hundred and twenty-five dollars!" My eyes nearly popped out of my head as I thrust the tube back at her.

Samantha didn't bat an eye. "That's because it works. Take it." She pushed my hand with the tube in it back toward me and I looked down at it again.

"I don't know, Samantha. It's your mom's. And it was so expensive."

Samantha sighed heavily. "My mum spends a fortune, especially on her skin. She's got to. It's her livelihood—she's hosting the news every night. She has oodles of this stuff, in every house we own, and she can always get more. Our house manager in London handles all her prescriptions. He probably has more stockpiled, even. Don't worry!"

Samantha's mom was a model-turned-newscaster from Africa as well as a major public figure. She was married to an important billionaire businessman from Israel, and the two were in the press a lot for their charity work and hobnobbing with celebrities. Mrs. Frankel's dark skin was smooth and unlined, and she positively glowed from the TV set whenever I saw her on CNN. It would be nice to have skin like hers, which Samantha did, though lighter.

I sighed and looked down at the cream again. Maybe it had magic powers and would take me a step closer to my lifelong dream: being on TV or film. "Okay. Thank you so much. I'll try it."

"Okay, try it now!" she encouraged.

"Um, all right." I opened the tube and turned to look in the mirror to apply it and gasped at what I saw. I'd avoided mirrors since yesterday and had worn my baseball hat pulled low and my scarf pulled high, with my hair down over my cheeks, today for school. Jenna had asked me at lunch if I was in the witness protection program, and Piper had passed me in the hall without recognizing me.

But now, the lights were super bright in here, and I was shocked to see how bad my face looked. It was bright red and puffy and covered in swirly red scratches all over. I winced.

"Ay, Díos mio," I said, squeezing a blob of the thick emollient onto my hand and lightly smoothing a pea-sized amount of it onto my cheek. I paused, waiting for it to burn or itch, but it only felt cool and soothing. "Ah," I sighed.

Samantha nodded encouragingly. "It's for burn victims."

"Oh!" I felt a spasm of guilt at using this precious stuff for such a silly reason, but the cream felt so good on my face that I went ahead with it. Soon my whole face was lightly slathered in the shiny, yellowish concoction. It was so ugly, it must be working!

Samantha inspected my face and nodded in approval. "Excellent. You'll see. It's quite effective."

I handed the tube back to her. "Thank you."

But she shook her head. "Keep it."

I pursed my lips but agreed. "Thanks."

Heading out, I looked out the windows at the beach. It had been a while since I'd been upstairs in the Frankel house, and you had to really be on the second floor to realize how close you were to the water here. The first floor was sort of nestled in the dunes but the second floor— well, it felt like we were looming over the ocean, as if we were on a giant ship. I paused as we trotted back down the stairs, and I gazed out again over the beach below. The waves weren't too big—despite all the talk that a hurricane was brewing. It would pass us over, for sure, the way all the other ones always have. No problem.

Samantha, noticing I wasn't behind her, stopped and looked back up at me. "Pretty close to the water, right?" she said.

I nodded. "Beautiful." And I resumed my walk down the stairs.

"Yes, but I mean...what do you think about the storm coming?"

"Oh, come on. It's nothing. They always miss us."

Samantha bit her lip thoughtfully as we turned out all the lights. "I hope you're right. This is the only one of our houses that I truly love. I'd hate to see something happen to it. I was in a typhoon once in Bali, and a lot of the houses on the shore got washed away."

"I know I'm right," I said, with totally fake confidence (I really am a good actor). "How could I be wrong, with a face like this?" and we both laughed, but her comments had chilled me a little.

The knock came early the next morning, and it was so loud that it woke me up. It was still pretty dark out, but when I looked at my clock, I saw that it was already seven o'clock. Peering out from behind my curtain, I noticed a heavily clouded sky and an unfamiliar pickup truck in the drive-way, Then I heard male voices downstairs—my papí's and someone else's. *Were they here for Samantha*, I wondered? *Could her father have come to get her finally?* (Would he be driving a *pickup*?) Quickly, I popped out of my bed and went to the top of the stairs to listen.

"...the whole neighborhood, by five o'clock today," an unfamiliar man's voice was saying.

My mamí came out of her room just then, dressed for the day in her school clothes; she is getting her CPA—that's a degree to become a certified public accountant, which is a really big deal—and on Fridays she has classes up the Cape at her school. She and I looked at each other, perplexed. She pointed downstairs and mouthed the word for *who* at me in Spanish. I motioned that I didn't know and shrugged. We stood and listened.

"And you want us to go where?" my papí was asking.

"The middle school. The Red Cross is bringing in cots and supplies, and we're gonna put everyone up for the night. It's for your own safety and also the safety of the rescuers, so people don't have to come out in the storm to save anyone. We want you out of harm's way in advance, and these here houses are about the most vulnerable in town, maybe on the whole Cape. You've got some big old trees around the property too. Those could be at risk of falling on your house or snapping a power line and starting a fire."

"Thank you, Mr., uh…" My papí was terrible with names, especially American ones, which he often had trouble pronouncing with his Ecuadorian accent.

"Slater. Bud Slater. Chief Lifeguard for the town. I'm heading up the evacuation."

"Thank you, Mr. Slater. I will speak with my wife and we will decide. We have a responsibility to the house, to the Frankels, to watch over everything, so I'm not sure…" my papí trailed off.

"Right. But you can't very well look after their house if you're dead," said Mr. Slater.

Dead? My whole body went cold, and my stomach clenched in fear. *Dead?* I looked at my mamí and she shook her head vehemently, making a dismissive gesture that said, *Don't believe this guy.*

But my papí laughed and then Slater laughed.

"Right. Thank you," my papí said.

"All right. On my way. Just remember, the middle school doors open at two o'clock. I look forward to seeing you there tonight," said Mr. Slater. Then the door closed.

"Ramón?" my mamí called to my papí as she jogged down the stairs.

My parents began murmuring, and I couldn't make out anything else. I headed into the bathroom and flipped on the light to check out my face.

"Wow!" I whispered. My skin was no longer inflamed—it was back to its normal olive tone, and it wasn't puffy anymore. However, the red scratches were still there. They were scabbing over and were almost more obvious now. It looked like I'd had some elaborate red pattern tattooed all over my face.

"Ay, Díos!" I wailed, and I turned the light off again so

I wouldn't have to see my face as clearly. I just had to get through school today—maybe they'd even send us home early!—and then I could hide for the entire weekend. Thank goodness my papí wouldn't evacuate. There was no way I was spending any more time at my school than I had to—especially not with my face looking like this!

CHAPTER 7

Piper

The footsteps on the Petries' porch had belonged to a man named Bud Slater, and he had totally busted me.

Well, actually, he'd jumped when he'd found me standing there, frozen in place, on the porch.

"Oh my gosh, you startled me!" he'd said breathlessly. "I thought you were a ghost at first, haha!" he'd laughed. "You looked like my sister, who's long gone from here!"

I had just leaped to my feet when I'd heard his tread and had been looking around for somewhere to hide, but there hadn't been time. My face had flamed, and my body had gone cold when I saw him, but I hadn't known what to say—my tongue had been tied from embarrassment.

"Who are you?" he'd asked, not unkindly.

"I... I'm Piper. I'm a friend of Campbells," I'd stammered. Was he going to turn me in? Call the cops on me for trespassing?

But instead he'd just nodded. "Homesick for your friend?" he'd asked kindly.

Homesick for this house, I'd wanted to say, but hadn't. Instead, I'd nodded back at him, making a move to leave.

"I'm Bud Slater." He'd stuck out his hand and I'd shaken it. "I'm an old friend of Bill Petrie's, and I keep an eye on the house for them when they're not here. Oftentimes, I do just what you're doing. I come here just to be on the porch and watch the water. It's so peaceful." He'd turned to lean on the low shingled wall of the porch, resting his weight on his hands as he'd gazed out at the ocean. "Reminds me of when I was a kid..." He'd been thoughtful for a minute, and I hadn't been sure if I should stay or go, but then he'd seemed to come back to his senses.

"I can't believe how much the beach has eroded along here. Used to have a huge stretch of sand between this porch and the water... Now, well, it's like you could jump off the porch and right into the water, almost."

I nodded. "We learned about coastal erosion in science last year. We took a field trip to Osprey Beach up the street to see the damage and everything that was being done to try to protect the dunes to keep the beach from washing away."

Mr. Slater nodded. "It's an ongoing battle. Planting beach grass, putting in netting and blankets to hold the sand in place. One guy out in P-town even buried a buncha cars under his dune, to try to bulk it up. Not sure *that's* so great for the environment. And the hurricanes, well, they just eat away these beaches in big chunks. Speaking of which..." He'd lifted his hands and clapped them together. "Big storm coming! Gotta get ready! Are you ready?"

"Yes, I think so. It's kind of up to my grandma."

"Well, I hope you and your grandma keep safe in the storm, and just know that the Petries wouldn't mind you being here. It's a great spot for daydreaming and reminiscing," he'd said kindly.

"Okay, bye!" I'd spun on my heel, run to my bike, and pedaled home as quickly as I could. I'd never looked back. I'd been so mortified; I hadn't even told my friends about it at school yesterday. I might have told my mom, if she was here, but it was too much to explain on the phone or in a text. I *certainly* hadn't told my grandma, Bett, who had no use for people wasting time daydreaming like that.

Today, they'd let us out of school early so they could start getting ready to host the "evacuees," the people who would have to leave their houses and shelter there for the storm. It was for the best that they let us out of school anyway, because the storm was all any of us kids could talk about all morning. The day was dark and windy, though still warm, and the rain threatened but did not arrive before dismissal. Everyone was chattering about the evacuation and supplies and storm surges and power outages and all kinds of things. I'd hear one kid saying that we were getting hit for sure, by six o'clock tonight, but then another kid would say, "Oh, no, it's swerving already. We won't get more than a little rain." It was really hard to know what would happen.

When they let us go, my friends and I went our separate ways, even though we truly wanted to hang out. Everyone's parents wanted them to go straight home to help them get ready for the storm. I hadn't heard from Bett, but I pretended that I had. It was less embarrassing that way. The truth was, my mom *had* texted me about the hurricane— she'd seen something about it on the news where she lived. But I tried to call her, and she didn't pick up.

When I got home from school, all was chaos at the farm. There were around a dozen horse trailers pulled up and parked at awkward angles all over the grass in front of the stables. Unfamiliar adults were milling around, and also my uncle Jack who had come up from Truro to help. Horses were whinnying, and Bett was marching around in her tan work jodhpurs and black rubber boots, barking into her cell phone. For a split second, I considered heading back to the house to hide in my room, but if Bett had drilled one thing into me it was, *Farm people help each other.* So, I took a deep breath and headed into the fray.

There were volunteers from up the Cape and down the Cape and inland who were picking up horses to board during the storm. There were owners from all over the place, either checking on their horses or shuttling them away in the trailers to higher ground.

Our farm lies at sea level right along the water, which

is a huge plus, according to Bett. People pay top dollar to be able to see the water when they ride in our rings—it's cooler here than inland, for one thing, and it feels so open and spacious—just like the old days on the Cape, says Bett, before all the crowds got so out of hand. Also, we offer guided trail rides over the dunes and along the beach, using our own horses, and that's a good source of income for us in the summer. This summer, Bett even let me lead a bunch of trail rides myself, which I loved. I made a lot of money in tips off that, much more than usual. I realized this summer that money in the bank makes me feel safe. I've got to make more as soon as I can.

"Woo! Feel that wind!" said my uncle Jack with a grin, as he led a big bay horse out of the barn. The wind buffeted me, and the gust felt like it could almost knock me over. It had really picked up since I'd left for school this morning, and it was extra strong here with nothing between me and the ocean except open land.

"And look at the sea," agreed another man—one of

the drivers—as he directed a spotted paint pony onto a trailer.

I turned to look out at the water, and I couldn't believe how much it had changed in just two days. There were tons of whitecaps on its dark gray surface now, and the wind was whipping it into a froth. The waves weren't too big yet, but I heard someone behind me saying with urgency that we were expecting an eight-to-ten-foot swell tonight. Eight-foot waves were huge! Like, practically Hawaii!

I turned around and saw that it was the man I'd met on the Petries' porch talking to Bett. She'd hung up her phone and was focused intently on what he was saying.

"Bett, that water's coming clear up here. You've gotta evacuate." He was standing with two teenagers in red life-guard shirts. I recognized them from Lookout Beach where they worked during the summer. One of them was soooo cute. He was shorter than I am, though, and older. But he had dimples and the whitest teeth when he smiled. I think lifeguards are so brave. Now here were two of them at my very own home. I like to swim in the ocean, but I'd be so scared to go in and try to save someone. Plus, I don't really like being in a bathing suit in front of people anymore.

Bett's chin tipped out, and I knew that was her stubborn look. "Bud, I appreciate what you're saying, and I vow to you now that I won't call for help so as not to endanger any potential rescuers. But I am *not* leaving. I've lived here my whole life, and that house is far enough off the beach and well protected in that little dip—we're snug and low. Nothing happened to it in 1938, nothing happened to it in '91, and nothing will happen to it now. We've got no big trees right around the place to fall on us, and I've got plenty of candles. I'm not going anywhere. You can't make me."

Bud put his hands up in a gesture of surrender and laughed. "Okay, okay, easy there, tiger. Look, you do what you've got to do. But don't try to be a hero, Bett. Human life's worth more than horses, no matter what you say. You've got my cell number if you need me, and the middle school doors will be open all night if you change your mind. Take care of yourself, pal." He patted her on the back, and she nodded firmly once, and he walked off to his truck. When he turned and hopped up into the cab, he spotted me watching him and he gave me a smile and a wave. I waved back, but I didn't smile. I was still embarrassed about our meeting the other day.

I turned to Bett who was muttering, "Most horses' lives are worth more than most humans, that's for darn sure!"

I laughed. "Oh, Bett. What can I do to help?"

She looked at me as if just seeing me. "Piper! Honey! Hi. What are you doing home so early?"

I explained how she'd probably gotten a text from my school saying that they'd let us out at noon so they could transform the school into a shelter, and that I'd ridden my bike home. She didn't ask if I'd eaten lunch yet (I hadn't), and I didn't mention it. That wasn't really Bett's thing. I'm sure she figured that if I were hungry, I'd eat, and that I'd know where to get the food when I needed it, and I guess she was right.

"Oh, Piper. Let's see. Could you do a walk-through of all the stalls and let me know who's still in there? I've got to call an owner back and the reception is terrible in there. Just do an inventory and come right back. Thanks."

Inside the barn it was dark, damp, and windy, and though there were only a few horses left—five to be exact—you could sense their nervousness. There was lots of stomping in their stalls, and you could hear some snorting and lots of hard air-blowing coming from their noses. I stopped in to see my horse, Buttercup, and give her a scratch, but she wouldn't even come to the door. She was cowering in the corner of her stall.

"Oh, Cuppie, I'm so sorry horsie. It'll all be over soon," I cooed at her, but she was having none of it. She blew a great puff of air hard out of her nose and tossed her head, moving restlessly in place.

I made a mental note of all the horses so I could tell Bett

who was left, and then I promised them I'd come back with carrots and apples later. The ones who were staying—at least three of these were ours so would likely stay—would need some comforting for sure.

Outside, Bett was still barking into her phone about pickups and guarantees and what was covered by flood insurance, so I tuned her out. Coming down the driveway was a big, beautiful, shiny black Range Rover—an unusual sight on the Cape in general, but a real rarity in the off-season—so I stood and admired its approach while I waited for Bett to get off the phone. Range Rovers are sooo much nicer than the gross pickup and the beat-up old Ford that Bett has. One day, if I worked really hard, I'd buy one of those, I promised myself.

Funnily enough, the Petries owned a gorgeous black Range Rover, and it made me think of them now. I wondered if Mr. and Mrs. Petrie had to do anything to get ready for the storm in Boston. I wondered if their housekeepers and houseman up in Boston had to do a lot to ready their townhouse in Beacon Hill. I wondered what *that* house was like and if I'd ever get to see it.

Right as the Range Rover drew up, the back door flung open and someone called my name. It *was* the Petries—Campbell and her parents! I ran to the side of the car.

"Cammie!" I cried, throwing my arms around her.

"Piper!" she cried back. We hugged and rocked back and forth in happiness.

Mr. and Mrs. Petrie came out to say hi, both of them hugging me, and asking how I was, how was school, were we ready for the storm, and where was Bett.

I pointed Bett out to them, and they left me and Campbell to chat. It had only been ten days since we'd seen each other, but it felt like ages. The words couldn't come out fast enough.

"How's Buttercup?" Campbell asked.

"How's Jagger?" I replied, as we talked over each other in our excitement about school, horses, pets, and more.

"I had no idea you were coming back!" I said finally.

Campbell nodded. "I know. I didn't either. It was kinda

spontaneous. A guy named Mr. Slater watches the house for us here, but there's no one to stay in it overnight. My parents were so worried it might get damaged that they decided we'd better just come down and stay here ourselves. They picked me up at school with the car already packed, and we came straight down."

"Awesome. When are you here until?"

"I think just till the storm passes. Sunday?"

I nodded as she looked around.

"Do you think it's going to hit?" she asked.

"Mmm, I really don't know. Everyone's acting like it, though."

The wind blew hard for a minute, and Campbell hugged her arms around herself. "I'm scared to stay at our house. I don't want to get washed away."

"Oh, haha! Funny. Washed away!" I laughed, but then I saw that Campbell was scared for real, and I flashed back to my conversation on their porch with Mr. Slater about beach erosion. "Wait, are you really scared?"

She nodded, her blue eyes huge. "Haven't you seen all those hurricane videos on YouTube, of the storms down south? People's entire houses get washed away by waves. People are rowing boats down the street. People *die*."

"Oh. Well... I don't think that will happen here." I said, feeling uneasy now. I looked around and pictured waves washing my house away while I rowed a boat down the driveway. "We don't even have a boat!" I said, all feisty and confident, but I was faking it for Campbell's sake, and she knew it.

She sighed and looked unhappy. "I'm psyched to see you, but I really wish we hadn't come. And my brother and sister are away at boarding school, so it's just me and my parents in that whole house. I hate it when it's just the three of us. I get so scared all alone in my wing of the house."

"I can stay with you!" I practically jumped at the chance. *Oh, to be in that house again! That's what matters!*

Campbell smiled for the first time in a few minutes. "Really? That would be awesome!"

I nodded, glad to relieve her anxiety but more importantly, ecstatic at the idea of getting in there again. I wondered if the cook or housekeeper would be coming in! "Let's go tell Bett."

Bett was busy chatting with the Petries and fielding phone calls. I interrupted politely to give her the list of the remaining horses and she nodded, saying that four would be staying here for the storm and that left only one last horse to be picked up, which should happen within the hour. "Thanks, Piper. Good work."

"Anything else?" I asked, hoping she'd say no.

She bunched her lips together for a second then said, "Nope. I think we're good for the moment."

"Great! So, can I go sleep over at Campbell's?" I asked, feeling exhilarated.

Bett's face grew perplexed. "No, sweetheart. I'm sorry. I need you here."

"But...you just said..."

Heading off an awkward moment, Mrs. Petrie stepped

in and said, "I know how busy you are, Bett, so we'll just head out and let you two chat. Please let us know if you need anything and just know that Piper's welcome anytime. I'm happy to come back to pick her up."

Campbell was looking at me sadly, but I was furious. "Thank you, Mrs. Petrie," I said through gritted teeth. I'd been taught to never forget my manners, no matter how I felt.

"Bye, honey!" said Mr. Petrie. "So long, Bett. And good luck."

"Bye now," said Bett with a brisk nod, her mind already elsewhere.

I wheeled on Bett once the Petries were out of earshot. "Why can't I go? You don't need me here. You've got Uncle Jack and it looks like plenty of other help." *My mother would let me go!* I wanted to scream but didn't.

Bett stared daggers at me. "If you think I'd let you out of my sight when they're predicting winds of up to one hundred miles an hour and waves up to ten feet, not to mention five inches of rain and extraordinary flooding, then we must never have met, missy. And that house of cards they live in—that old Slater place—it's going right down, mark my words. Sleep over at the Petries', well I never! Your mother would never forgive me if something happened to you on my watch! Jack! Jacky!" Bett wandered away, calling out to my uncle.

I stood there in shock, not because of all the weather predictions she'd just thrown at me—though those were scary enough—or the fact that she'd referred to it as the old Slater place (like, as in Bud Slater?), but because I was speechless at the idea of anything happening to the Petries' house. (Oh yes, and, of course, the Petries!)

Could the Petrie/Slater house actually be at risk of washing away?

CHAPTER 8

Ziggy

FRIDAY AFTERNOON

*Oh man, I am so stressed out. Like, I need to do some medi-*tating and maybe take a soak in a hot bath with some Epsom salts, or a steam out in our homemade sauna. I've had a crazy afternoon. Well, it started out as just a busy afternoon, and then it got crazy—and weird.

So, they let us out of school early today for the hurri-cane, and I was psyched because I had so much to do, and this just meant we would have some extra time. My dad and I had talked about going over to the food bank today to see if we could help with any storm prep, and I wanted to stop by the Nature Conservancy office at Lookout Beach to see if they needed me to do anything with animal protection or securing the endangered piping plover bird habitats. I'd also wanted to check on all my knitting club friends and make sure they had what they needed.

I'd called my dad from the school office to come and get me, and I'd heard my mom yelling in the background, "School's *out*? Oh, so they've bought into the hype too? When will this end?"

Luckily, my dad had left her at home and zoomed over solo in the Prius to get me, arriving just ten minutes later. We set out for the food bank, which is in a strip mall on the edge of town. In the back of the car, I spotted cartons of lettuce from our garden, along with dozens of fresh eggs and little boxes of green beans.

"You must've been out there picking all morning!"

I said to my dad. I was impressed at how much he had accomplished.

He nodded. "Anything I left behind would have been ruined by the storm, so I took everything, but your mother was not happy with me. She talked me into leaving behind the tomatoes."

I looked straight ahead at the road and kept my voice neutral. "What did she say?"

My dad sighed. "Mom thought I was buying into the storm hype, but we agreed to disagree." He turned to look at me. "I'm sorry your mother is acting so funny about this storm. I think she's just scared and doesn't want to face her fears, so she gets angry to hide it or handle it or something."

I raised my eyebrows. "It's pretty weird. I mean, look around." I gestured to the shops we were passing in town—many of which had boarded up their windows or duct-taped giant Xs across them to keep the glass from shattering. No one was on the street and everything was closed. Westham was a ghost town. "Everyone else thinks it's happening."

He nodded. "I know. Let's just do what we need to do to be safe and ready, and your mom will come along in the end, okay?"

"Are we going to evacuate?" I asked. I half-wanted to because it would be kind of exciting, but I also didn't want to have to leave our cozy little house and sleep in my school!

"I'm going to make that decision later today." He piloted the car into the parking lot and turned into an empty spot—they were almost all empty today, which was *very* unusual—and we began unloading the car.

Inside the food pantry, the shelves were pretty bare. Marisol, the director of the pantry, greeted us with open arms as usual. Sometimes I like to pretend she's my grandma because she's what I would want in a grandma— small, white-haired, huggy, always smiling, always offering food, and always smelling delicious, like cinnamon and cloves.

"It's time for happiness to bloom!" she said, sweeping me into a warm hug. She always says that when we arrive because of our last name. (Bloom, get it?)

"Hi, Mari!" I said into her shoulder.

She held me at arm's length and beamed at me. "There's my girl! So beautiful! Growing up so fast!"

She hugged my dad and asked after my mom, and then they began discussing the hurricane.

"We've been totally drained," she said, gesturing to the nearly empty shelves. "We had lines out the door this morning, but I'm worried about the people who *didn't* come. I've got four elderly ladies who usually come on Saturdays, but they won't be able to get in here tomorrow, and they've got to be running low on supplies."

"Will you let us bring them a delivery?" asked my dad. "Or is that an invasion of privacy?"

Marisol considered it for a moment. "Well, I think it would be a great idea. You could also see if they'd like a ride to the shelter, though I don't think any of them will.

I would do it myself, but I've got to stay here until closing time at least, and that's seven p.m. Are you sure you don't mind?"

My dad was scanning the almost-bare shelves with his eyes. "No, we don't mind at all, and the rides would be fine. It's just that there isn't a lot here."

Marisol was already gathering cardboard delivery boxes. She laid out four of them on the metal table and quickly began sorting through the remaining items and putting things into them. "Hang on. I've got to hit the emergency rations," she said, ducking into her office in the back of the small warehouse.

My dad and I looked at each other and smiled. "I thought these *were* the emergency rations," he said, and we laughed.

Marisol returned with four boxes of Minute Rice, four cans of chicken noodle soup, and four small jars of peanut butter, all balanced in her arms. She had a package of sandwich bread hooked over her thumb, and she opened the bag and doled out four slices each into four Ziploc bags. Though I winced at the single-use plastic bags (terrible for the environment, especially sea creatures), I thought it was pretty clever of Marisol to stretch the food like that. My dad added in a head of lettuce for each box, then he used his pocketknife to cut the egg cartons into four-egg size and sorted those into the boxes. Finally, he used some of the ziplock bags too and gave each box a hefty handful of green beans. He put the rest of the produce and eggs into the walk-in cooler for other people to select, and we were ready.

"Wait!" said Marisol. She darted back to her office and then returned, grinning sheepishly as she ripped open a bag of Halloween candy. "People need treats in a crisis. Now, let me write down the names and addresses for you. I'll have them ready by the time you're finished loading your car."

Soon we were on our way. I read over the list and directed my dad.

The first lady lived out on Route 28, a busy section of highway, and there wasn't a car in her small driveway. I wondered how she got anywhere from there—she would be stranded without a car. But her house was pleasant, and she was thrilled to see us. "Oh, I kept meaning to call a taxi to take me over there for some food, and then I just kept getting too busy!"

I couldn't imagine what was keeping her so busy, but I didn't ask.

My dad offered to help with any storm prep or to take her to the shelter, but she declined. "My granddaughters are coming to sleep over once they get off work today—which should be soon—so I am all set and looking forward to that, but thank you, young man. I do appreciate all the help!"

I was happy to hear she had family coming and wouldn't be all alone or stranded for the storm. It made leaving her easier.

The next lady's house was closed and dark and locked

up tight, so we kept her box, and reported back to Marisol that she had evacuated. Marisol said to give the extra box to someone else.

At the third house, we found it bustling and the lady was very happy to see us, but she was busy and distracted. She had people of all ages there—her son and daughter, their spouses, a bunch of teenagers, and some little kids—and they were all staying with her for the hurricane because they'd been evacuated.

"Looks like a house party!" said my dad.

"I know! It's a family reunion!" joked the lady, as her son gratefully accepted the box plus the extra one we hadn't placed at the previous stop.

The last stop was the hard one. The lady, Mrs. MacNichol, was all alone, and she was scared. She was worried that her power would go out and she'd fall when she got up to go to the bathroom. She had no food or water or flashlights for the storm, no one to check on her, and my father finally talked her into evacuating to the school. I helped her stash the food and pack her things in a shopping bag, and she worried all the way to the school about how she would get home after the storm. My dad promised her that we would drive her home, and she relaxed after that.

My dad brought her in to the shelter while I called Marisol to explain and let her know we'd dropped the extra box off. When my dad got back in the car, he said the school nurse was helping Mrs. MacNichol, and she'd spotted a friend and some acquaintances and seemed to be happy to be there.

Now he turned the car to head to the Nature Conservancy office at Lookout Beach, and I took a deep, cleansing breath and let it out.

"Okay, Zigs?" asked my dad.

"Yeah, but it's a lot. I felt bad for Mrs. MacNichol. The other ladies had family coming or already there, and it made a huge difference. She was all on her own."

"Mmm-hmm," my dad's face looked like he was miles away.

"It seems like family really helps in a crisis," I said, looking out the window as we passed Brookfield Lane, where Selena lived.

My dad made a kind of gasping sound, like he was crying, and I turned quickly to look at him. "Are you okay?" I asked.

He cleared his throat. "Yes. Sorry. Just had a little tickle in my throat." But his eyes were kind of watery. I looked at him suspiciously.

"Do you miss your parents?" I asked. We'd reached the top of the beach parking lot and he stopped the car.

He turned to me with a shocked look on his face. "What?"

His surprise made me feel surprised. "What?" I asked.

"What made you ask about my parents just now?" he asked me, his eyebrows knitting together in confusion.

"Um, because we were talking about family and we just visited a bunch of old people who have families, weirdy," I teased, trying to lighten the mood. "Are you coming in?"

My dad looked out at the ocean, which was really choppy, with foam going every which way. The sand was blowing across the beach, and the lifeguard stands had been tipped over and dragged up to the dunes to protect them. He seemed to be thinking it over. Then he said, "I'm going to run a quick errand. I'll be right back."

"Okay," I agreed, hopping out.

I watched as he backed up and drove away, then I began to walk to the big beach pavilion that housed the Nature Conservancy office. I looked back at the last minute before climbing the stairs to the porch, and I saw my dad turn left on Brookfield Lane.

Huh. That was weird. What kind of an errand could he be doing there? It was just a street of oceanfront mansions—no stores or anything. And other than the Diazes, we sure didn't know any of the rich people who lived there.

Lost in thought, I crossed the porch, leaning into the wind, and pushed open the heavy door, which was warped with ocean dampness and stuck horribly. My friend Kathy was sitting at her desk, working at her computer, and no one was at the other desks in the shared office.

"Ziggy!" she turned as she heard the door groan open, and she smiled warmly at me. "How are you, my dear?"

"Hi, Kathy. I'm good. I came to see if you need help with the plover birds or anything?"

"That is so thoughtful, Ziggy, but we are in great shape. The final fledglings flew away last week, and the nests have all blown away in due course, as usual. I know we'll need your help when the storm is over, though. The beach cleanup could take days."

"Right!" I agreed. "I'll definitely..."

The door banged open and an oldish dude with gray hair came in, full of energy.

"Hi, Bud," said Kathy.

"Hey, Kathy. Shouldn't you be heading home? I've been all over town evacuating people all day, and the shelter is starting to fill up. Things are looking good down there. I think we should lock up and put some sandbags at the door. I was just coming in to lift some of the boxes of life-guarding files off the floor in case it floods in here."

"Hmm, good idea, actually," Kathy said.

I loved how organized and prepared this Bud guy was. He wasn't waffling about weather predictions or suspecting the government of conspiracy. He was just taking a stand and getting things done! "Do you need help?" I offered, hoping he'd say yes so I could join his crusade.

The Bud guy smiled at me. "No thanks, but I really appreciate you asking. Come see me next summer, though. We could use some doers like you in the Junior Lifeguards program. For now, though, you ought to get on home, kiddo. With this wind blowing, it isn't safe to be on the roads anymore."

Kathy agreed with him. "I agree. You should get going, Ziggy. I'm all set, honey. Thank you so much."

"Okay. Good luck everyone!" I said, and I left.

Back at the parking lot, there was no sign of my dad. He had probably assumed I'd be there for a while and so wouldn't be back too soon. The wind lifted my hair every which way—it would be murder to untangle it later—and the warm, damp air made my curls feel wet. I sat on the split rail fence at the top of the parking lot and leaned into the wind as I looked at the beach. It was wild and beautiful, actually. The waves were getting big and crashing against each other every which way, with arcs of white foam sailing through the air. The beach grass was bent nearly sideways in the wind, and seagulls were hanging in place in the sky, not even flapping their wings—just coasting on the gusts of air. The sky was blanketed with thick and low steel gray clouds, and you could almost taste the salt in the air from the seawater. Nature was beautiful, even in a crisis. I took deep breaths and tried to be very present, so I'd remember this moment always.

I turned to look at the trees down the road behind me and saw their branches were waving crazily, like someone calling for help in a panic, arms in the air. The wind was ripping leaves off the trees and blowing them in drifts along the road. *There were sure to be branches or even whole trees down all over town before the storm was through*, I thought absentmindedly. Hmm, maybe nature isn't always so beautiful. Maybe it's sometimes kinda scary.

I turned back to study the ocean some more and suddenly heard a huge crack and a crashing sound. I whipped back around. I'd been right—a massive old tree on the corner of Brookfield Lane had just come down. But right next to it was a car—our car! I jumped off the fence and began running down the hill.

CHAPTER 9

Jenna

FRIDAY AFTERNOON

*Franny Barnes's parents had come to watch the end of prac-*tice yesterday. I'd overheard them telling Coach Randall that they were leaving straight from the Y pool to head up to Salem to spend two nights up there, so they'd be fresh for the regional tournament tomorrow. At the end of practice, perfect Franny rushed out, and she and her perfect parents got into their perfect car and rushed off to Salem, where I was sure she'd swim perfectly and beat me in the rankings once and for all. I stood there dripping and furious and watched them go.

The regional tournament had still not been canceled as of noon today, but Coach Randall had sent out a text today when she heard school was canceled and invited anyone in for an optional practice today. Since *optional* means *required* in my family, I went.

The first thing Coach Randall did this afternoon was to tell us all that she would not be going to the regional tournament, and she did not expect any of us to be there.

"In fact, I think it's dangerous and irresponsible that they haven't canceled it yet. This hurricane is going to hit and hit hard. I don't want any of you on the roads tomorrow," she said fiercely. "Better to stay home and play it safe."

"But what about all our training? And how will our state standings be affected if we don't post scores at the regionals?" I asked, picturing Franny's name at the top of the scoreboard.

Coach Randall's face was grim. "You'll retain your standing from the last quarter. The training is what it is; you'll just have to wait until the next regionals this winter."

I huffed in aggravation. This was so unfair!

I swam hard today—harder than usual, even though Coach Randall had told us to take it easy. I was angry and it helped. Afterward, I got dressed and was heading out to see who was picking me up when Coach Randall called to me from her office.

"Bowers? Come on in for a minute, please."

I entered her office and she gestured for me to shut the door and sit down.

"Jenna, I know this is disappointing for you. I know you've trained your heart out this summer and put a ton of effort into everything. It's hard for me too. I've seen all you girls improve so much, and the regionals were a great goal, an incentive, that motivated you all. In many ways, the meet has already served its purpose. I'm sorry they're not canceling it—it does seem unfair—but life goes on.

It's more important for you all to stay close to home, stick together with your family, and be safe. Between you and me, I didn't think it was smart for the Barneses to rush up there, but they have their own reasons for why they do things. I just wanted you to know I'm proud of you and that I know you would have killed it up there. That's all. Okay?"

I nodded sadly. "Thanks."

"Chin up, kid. Maybe there's a reason you're stuck here. Maybe it's all part of a bigger plan." She smiled. "Okay? There's always the next one." She stood up. "I'm heading out now. Do you need a ride?"

I thanked her and declined.

"I'm going to just do a run-though here and make sure everyone's out before I lock up. Is your family being evacuated?" she asked as we left her office.

"I don't think so," I said. "We're pretty far from any water."

"Same here," she agreed. "I might pop into the shelter to see if I can help with anything, though."

"Like what?" I asked.

"Oh, you know, moving beds, walking dogs outside, entertaining the kids, meal prep...whatever they need."

Huh. I hadn't thought of anything like that. "Good idea," I said. "Maybe my friends and I can help there too. I'm going to check with them."

"Atta girl! That's thinking like a winner!" said Coach Randall with a smile. "Good luck. Stay safe."

"Thanks. You too, Coach."

Outside, the wind was roaring, and my mom was waiting in her car. "Hi, honey. Can you believe this wind?" she asked as I hopped in and buckled up. I explained my plan to volunteer and my mom agreed. "All right, but not for too long. People have to be off the streets by six."

She waited while I contacted my friends, texting Selena and Piper and calling Ziggy's landline.

Ziggy's mom answered and said that Ziggy and her dad were still out, but that she'd have Ziggy call me when she came in.

"Any word from Selena or Piper?" asked my mom, her hands on the wheel, ready to go.

"Nope. Maybe we could go look at the ocean at Lookout Beach? It would give them a few more minutes to reply, and we'll be close enough to their houses to pick them up then."

My mom agreed and put the car in drive.

I sighed and sat back to look out the window as we drove. Town was empty and the rain was starting to come down now in a light spatter. A garbage can had blown over and was rolling across the sidewalk. Tree branches were already down, and leaves clogged the gutters at each corner.

"Oh, Mom, I am so bummed about this regionals thing. I just can't believe they didn't cancel it," I moaned, smacking my knees with open palms.

"I know. It's ridiculous," she agreed.

"And Franny Barnes is going, and she's going to pull ahead of me once and for all when she posts her new times."

My mom's face was a mask of disbelief. "The Barneses are going? Seriously? That's incredibly dangerous."

"Mm-hmm," I said. Yikes. "You really think it's that dangerous?"

She looked at me with wide eyes. "You should see the weather reports! This thing is heading square for us, and if you saw what it's already done elsewhere, well..." She caught herself suddenly. "I mean, we'll be fine. Don't worry. It's just. Wow. Those people are nuts!"

"Mom, are you scared?" I asked. Suddenly things were seeming really real around here.

"Well, I'm not scared exactly, but I'm not looking forward to it, you know?"

"Are we evacuating?"

She shook her head. "I think Granny and Grampy are coming over, and maybe some of my sisters and brothers, cousins, I'm not sure. We have space, and Ginny has a generator she can bring, so we were thinking it might be good to all stick together."

We were just coming around the curve at Ocean Road when we saw a Prius up ahead, and a huge tree limb down in front of it. My mom said, "Whoa!" and slowed down. The tree was almost totally blocking the road up to the beach, so she put on her hazard lights and stopped at an angle to the Prius.

"Let me just see if they're okay."

But right as she got out, I saw someone running toward the Prius from the beach—someone who looked a lot like...Ziggy?

I jumped out of the car and jogged over to the Prius, reaching it right as my mom and Ziggy did.

"Ziggy!" I called.

The door to the Prius opened and a shocked-looking Mr. Bloom got out, his face ashen.

"Josh, are you hurt?" asked my mom urgently.

Ziggy threw her arms around her dad. "Oh, Daddy! I thought you'd gotten crushed by the tree!"

"I'm—I'm okay," stuttered her dad, looking all around

as he patted Ziggy on the back absentmindedly. "Wow. That was a close call." The huge limb had just missed smashing his car by inches.

Suddenly a white-haired, tiny lady came running down the driveway of the big white mansion on the corner. "Joshie? Are you okay?"

He turned, looked shocked to see her, and waved her off. "I'm fine. Thank you! All set! You should go back inside where it's safe!"

We all looked at the lady who was peering anxiously at him from the end of the driveway. She looked like she wanted to come over to him, but something was stopping her. She wrung her hands and just watched. How did she know his name, I wondered? And *Joshie*?

"Who's that lady?" Ziggy asked her dad. "How do you know her?"

The lady looked wretchedly upset. She hugged her arms around herself, and she and Ziggy stared at each other for a minute, then Ziggy's dad said, "Let's get this branch off the road before someone comes around the corner and hits it. Girls, you stay here. Meg, do you mind helping me?"

My mom and Mr. Bloom dragged the branch safely to the side of the road while the lady continued to watch us from the mansion's driveway. Ziggy kept stealing looks at her, alternating with watching our parents.

"Want to go volunteer at the shelter with me?" I asked.

Ziggy looked at me, interested. "I was there earlier. Sure. Let me ask my dad. When would you want to go?"

I shrugged. "Now?" It was four thirty. "We could see if Selena's home and wants to come?"

"Okay."

It took a few minutes organizing, plus convincing Selena that her face wasn't that bad anymore, before we were all in my mom's car and headed to the shelter. Piper couldn't come, but Selena's mom had asked us to take Samantha

Frankel along with us, since she was now staying in the Diazes' house, so there were four of us. Samantha was worked up because this was her first hurricane, though she'd been in a typhoon in Bali once and an earthquake in Bolivia.

"Boy, you sure get around!" said Ziggy. "Lucky! Except for the carbon footprint."

"Yes. But I'm nervous for this experience, even if I'm a little excited for it."

"I wouldn't say hurricanes are something to look forward to!" said my mom, but she smiled kindly at Samantha in the rearview mirror as she said it. "They're awfully damaging and dangerous once they hit."

"Oh, I know. It just makes for an interesting change, I guess. Everyone mucking in together, helping each other, looking out for each other." Samantha shrugged and looked out the window. She looked kind of sad.

My mom pulled up to the school and parked the car. "Okay, you girls have one hour. I'll be back at five thirty to bring you all home. After that, it's time to hunker down, okay?"

We all agreed and scurried through the light rain inside. Because of swim team, I was rarely in our school when it wasn't in session. I was surprised to realize it was actually kind of fun! Maybe that's part of why kids do extracurriculars. There was a table set up just inside the front door, and there were a bunch of high school kids stationed there, all in those red lifeguard tee shirts again. They were cool and impressive, seeming so old and professional to me.

"Hello! Are you evacuating?" asked one of the lifeguard girls, tossing her zillions of tiny braids over her shoulder as she leaned eagerly across the table and smiled at us.

I smiled back. "No, but thank you. We came to see if we could help out."

"Awesome!" said another one of the lifeguards, this was the same guy with blond hair and dimples and very white teeth who I'd seen the other day at the town docks.

He was really handsome, actually, even if he was too short for me. Considering that every guy my own age was too short for me, it wasn't saying much. He was super friendly, though, and came right over to us to chat. "I'll bring you in to see my dad. He's running things in general, and I'm sure he could use help somewhere," he said, coming around to the front side of the table. "Have you all volunteered anywhere before?"

We all began enumerating our volunteer experiences at once and he laughed, holding up his hands in surrender. "Okay, okay, I get it! You're all very active volunteers. That's great. That's what usually draws people to lifeguarding," he said.

"Are lifeguards volunteers?" I asked.

"Well, once you're a lifeguard, you do get paid for the work, but the training—the Junior Lifeguards program—is volunteer. Everyone has to do it to become a lifeguard in Westham. But what I meant was, lifeguards are usually people who like to help others. It's a very hands-on, concrete way to be helpful. You're literally saving people's lives sometimes."

"And risking your own," added the girl with the braids, from over his shoulder.

"Wow," I said. That sounded pretty major. I wanted to learn more.

Just then, the front door of the school opened and there was a hubbub of noise. I turned to see a news crew entering, shaking off raincoats, pulling plastic off their cameras and generally making a scene. One of them, a lady with tons of makeup and a snazzy raincoat, came to the table and introduced herself.

"I'm Tabitha Jones, Local News Seven. I'd love to come in and do a piece on how the evacuation's going, maybe interview a few people. Is now a good time?"

The first lifeguard stood and introduced herself, then offered to go check with Bud Slater to see what was allowed. "I'll be right back."

Selena clutched my arm. "I wish *I* could be interviewed!

This could have been my big Hollywood break! But not with this face like it is. I'm such an idiot!" She ducked her head in shame and pulled her baseball hat low and her scarf high. The truth was, her face really did look much better today. The scratches had started to flake off a little, and it wasn't as bad as it had been yesterday. But all that wasn't to say it looked good, because it didn't.

I patted her hand. "Don't worry, Leeny, you'll have bigger chances in life than Local News Seven during a dumb hurricane. This is not the stuff that Hollywood careers are made of."

The four of us walked to the gymnasium together, Selena turning four or five cartwheels down the hall, and the cute lifeguard guy and the lifeguard girl came too. They walked us over to Bud Slater (turns out the cute guy was his son) to see how we could volunteer. I was a little suspicious of Mr. Slater because my dad hadn't been wild about him earlier, but he was friendly and eager for our help. He assigned me and Selena to entertain some little kids for a while, and Ziggy and Samantha to walk dogs, sticking close to the school building and away from big trees. Then he agreed to let in the news crew because it would help get the word out about the shelter. He left to go meet Tabitha Jones.

The gymnasium was set up with cots in row after row—about half of them were taken so far. It looked like a huge Army barracks. Ziggy was saying hello to an old lady she knew, and Selena and I made a beeline over to the group of little kids who were running wild and shrieking.

Selena clapped her hands and called, "Singalong time!"

"Brilliant idea," I said.

The kids were bored, obviously, so they willingly formed a circle and Selena began to sing. She has a very good singing voice and a lot of presence. I do not have a *good* singing voice, but it is fine, so I sang quietly and let her take the lead.

In between the second and third song, a little girl said to Selena, "Why you hiding?"

"I'm sorry? What?" asked Selena.

"Why you hiding under that?" said the little girl, who was probably three.

"She means your hat and scarf," I said. "It does look a little weird."

Selena sighed. "I hurt my face, and it looks yucky," she said to the little girl. Now all the kids were transfixed.

"Let's see!" one voice shouted, but then it quickly turned into a chant from a chorus of voices.

Selena looked at me in desperation and I shrugged.

"Give the people what they want," I said. "It's not that bad."

Sighing, Selena lifted off the hat, slid the scarf off her neck, and shook her hair loose, over her shoulders. The kids cheered and the first little girl jumped up and came over to inspect Selena's face. Then a whole crowd of them joined in.

"You not look so bad," said the little girl wisely.

Selena smiled.

"How did you hurt your face? Was it from the hurricane?" asked a little boy with fear in his eyes.

"Oh, no, not at all!" said Selena. She looked at me with pain in her eyes, then turned back to them. "I was trying to make myself look pretty and I scrubbed too hard. It was dumb." She shrugged.

"You're already pretty!" said a little boy, then he blushed and ducked behind his brother.

"Yeah!" all the kids chorused. A new chant started up: "Prih-TY! Prih-TY!"

Selena laughed and clapped her hands. "Thanks, kids. Let's harness that energy into singing... 'I've Been Working on the Railroad!'"

As Selena sang and the kids joined in on every chorus, the camera crew started drawing near to us. I was actually having a lot of fun by this point, and so were the kids and Selena. The camera guy circled us and filmed us from behind; Selena would be safe from the prying eyes of the camera, for better or worse. After the song was over, Tabitha Jones came over, clapping her hands.

"Can I interview you girls on camera? Are you life-guards too?"

Selena blushed and tried to decline, admitting what she'd done to her skin. One of the camera guys said he could put a lens over his camera to soften the image so viewers wouldn't see her cuts. While this negotiating was going on, I saw a new family arrive in the doorway with their bags.

It was Franny Barnes and her parents.

CHAPTER 10

Selena

FRIDAY NIGHT

I was on TV tonight, and people saw it!

The news show filmed me and Jenna singing with the kids at the shelter (so nice not to be told to be quiet in school, btw!), and then the reporter interviewed us! I was worried because of my face, but the camera guy did a trick to hide it and it didn't look too bad after all. The reporter said I was a "natural." My phone started blowing up after the show aired at six, and I was able to do a screen grab with the video and put it on all my social media. I am so excited. Maybe someone will see it and make me a star!

That's the good news. The bad news is that we have to stay at the shelter tonight. My mamí, Hugo, and Samantha and me. My friends and I were just getting ready to leave after volunteering when I saw my family appear in the doorway of the gymnasium. They were each carrying a little bag, and my mamí had brought an extra one for me and one for Samantha. My papí was there too, but he was going to go back and stay in the Frankels' house in a maid's room, just to keep an eye on things. I didn't like the idea of him there at all. I immediately thought of that view of the swirling ocean out of the master bedroom window. How much closer might the water come? Could the whole house collapse into the water like I'd seen on YouTube from hurricanes elsewhere? We'd studied coastal erosion in science last year, and even though the reading was boring, the videos were wild.

"Papí, please don't! Please stay here with us!" I begged, hanging off him in a hug.

He patted me briskly. "Selena, this is my job, or one of them, anyway. I have a responsibility to the Frankels. I must be there. They *trust* me to be there. Okay? Be a good girl and look after your mamí for me."

He and my mamí shared a long hug, and he clapped Hugo on the shoulder before he left. "I'll see if I can get a chance to come back during the eye, but it might be the middle of the night."

My mamí nodded and smiled bravely at him "We'll be fine, amor. Cuidate. Take care of yourself."

"What's an eye?" I asked my mamí, as we made our way over to the cots to set up camp.

"A hurricane is a swirling ring of a storm. Picture a doughnut," she explained, gesturing with her fingers. "In the middle—the eye of the storm—it is perfectly empty and calm. There is no bad weather there, so it can give you a little break. Sometimes the sun even comes out and all the wind is gone. But you have to be careful, because the other side of the storm is still coming, just as strong as the first. You see?"

I nodded. "The doughnut hole is a trick. You still have to eat the other half."

She laughed. "Right. People can be very careless when the eye comes. They think the storm is over and they go down to look at the waves on the beach or something, and then...wham!"

I giggled because with my mamí's accent, "wham" came out as "uh-WOM." Still, it was scary to think about, and I did not like my papí back there in that big house, teetering on the dunes, all alone.

We picked four cots in a row and set down our things. The lifeguards were weaving around through the cots to see if people needed anything—toothbrushes, extra blankets, tea, or coffee. They said dinner would be soon. I liked the way the lifeguards were in charge, even though they were kids. They seemed so mature and confident, and they were all fit and cute-looking. They reminded me of the cast of a teen TV show. It looked like it would be fun to be a part of their group.

"Dinner at school!" I said to no one in particular. "This day just keeps getting weirder!"

Dinner was set up in the cafeteria at six thirty, and there was going to be a movie in the auditorium after—*Toy Story 2*, kinda babyish, but so what? It's important to learn about all kinds of productions if you're going to be a star one day like me. I read somewhere that animation is actually a really good part of the industry for actors to get into because you can voice your part from anywhere. Of course, I 'd rather be in *front* of the camera, but every bit of work helps!

"So, this is where you go to school?" asked Samantha, as we made our way through the cafeteria line with our trays. They'd set up pizzas and pasta and salad, and it wasn't too bad. The lifeguards in their red T-shirts were serving it from behind the counter. *What couldn't these kids do?* I marveled.

"Yep," I said. "I'm sure it's nowhere near as nice as your..." but then I caught myself. Samantha and I hadn't discussed why she was here. We'd barely even talked at all since she'd shared the healing cream with me the other night. Mostly, we'd just watched TV side by side on our couch. Now I had to acknowledge the fact that her arrival here was a little unusual. "Um. What's going on with your school?"

Samantha sighed. "Well, I loved my school back in London, but my parents took me out because I have some learning differences, and it was too hard for me. They heard about this supposedly great school in Massachusetts that helps dummies like me get better at school, but it was so far away. I didn't want to go."

I felt terrible for her. "You're not a dummy. Tons of kids have trouble in school. It has nothing to do with how *smart* you are."

Samantha rolled her eyes. "Right. But in a family of overachievers like mine, well..."

"So, what now?" We'd filled our trays and were following my mom and Hugo to a table full of strangers.

Samantha shrugged. "When the storm passes, I get the next plane home. But my parents will probably just drop me off somewhere else. Maybe it'll be on the same continent as them this time, though."

I thought it was a little strange that her parents hadn't come to get her, but what do I know about "overachievers," other than that they have huge fancy houses and live-in staff?

As we reached the table, I realized that not everyone there was a stranger. One of them was the school drama teacher, Mrs. Waters.

"Hi, Mrs. Waters," I said, putting my napkin on my lap as my mother looked on approvingly and then turned to chat with the lady next to her.

"Selena! Where have you been all week?" Mrs. Waters

asked in surprise. "I was expecting you to pick up your script on Wednesday and try out on Thursday!"

I blushed bright red. "I had a little mishap, and I wasn't able to come."

"But you were so excited to be in the play. I wish you had emailed me or come to see me. What happened?"

"I... I..." I wasn't sure what to say, so I blurted out the truth—the whole story of trying to give myself a home-made makeover to look my best for the audition, and how it backfired on me and I was only just healing.

Mrs. Waters was really nice about it. "Oh, Selena, honey, I don't know where to begin. First of all, you are a beautiful girl on the outside already, *and* on the inside, but it's the inside that I care about. It's the inside that audiences connect with. Looks only go so far—it's the talent and the authenticity, the honesty, that matters. And you've got that in spades! Oh, I wish you hadn't harmed yourself in the name of beauty, and I wish you'd come to tell me. We could have arranged a private audition. I thought you had changed your mind, so I cast the play without you in it."

I'd known that would be the case, but it still hurt to hear it.

Just then a girl from my grade came running over to the table. "Selena! You're on the news! Look!" She thrust an iPhone at me, and I caught a glimpse of myself just before it went to a commercial.

"No way!" I was so excited. "Gosh, that was so fast!"

People began trying to call it up on their phones and soon someone got it and we all gathered around to watch, even Mrs. Waters and the strangers at the table.

The news showed me and Jenna with the kids and then had a long clip of us singing "Puff the Magic Dragon." At the end, there was a clip of our interview, where Jenna and I were saying we were just doing our part, chipping in to help with the kids. Everyone applauded when the clip was over, and my mamí wanted to see it again.

"Selena, I didn't know you could sing so beautifully!" said Mrs. Waters.

"Oh, thanks. I love singing," I said modestly.

"Then I have just the play for you, my dear! Not to worry! I can certainly find a part of you in *It's a Wonderful Life*, the musical version. Rehearsals start November first. And no makeovers!" she wagged a finger at me. "I want you at auditions just as you are."

"But with less scratches on my face," I laughed.

"Right!"

"Selena! Come look at the storm!" One of the little kids from earlier had appeared by my side and was now pulling me over to a window that looked out on the street. When we reached it, I looked outside and gasped. The rain was now coming down in actual sheets, and the ground couldn't absorb it fast enough, so there were massive rivers running every which way. The wind was blowing so hard that the trees were bending practically in half, and branches and twigs were down everywhere.

"Oh no!" I gasped.

Suddenly, a lifeguard was there behind us. "You kids should stay away from the windows. Come," she said, and she led us back to our table in the middle of the room.

Right as I sat back down, there was a massive crash and the shatter of broken glass. A tree limb had just come through the very same window we'd been looking out not ten seconds earlier. The lifeguard had saved us!

"Díos mio!" I cried, as people shrieked.

And then the lights went out.

CHAPTER 11

Piper

FRIDAY NIGHT

We'd worked hard in the barn for the remainder of the afternoon—pitching as much dry hay as possible up to the loft to keep it from getting wet (this would be the horses' replacement bedding after the hurricane) and filling huge drums with fresh water, so that if the seawater got into our well and soured it during the storm, the horses would still have water to drink. We'd had to make sure all the barn's drains were free and clear so that any storm water would wash right down and not back up into the stalls and possibly drown the horses, and we'd gathered all the loose farm equipment—hoes, pitchforks, anything that the wind could pick up and throw—into a pile with bungee cords securing them down. My final job was to tag the four remaining horses with luggage ID tags that I'd braided into their tails; in case they got free and ran away, people would know who they belonged to. The warm, damp wind had whipped through the barn and the horses had grown more and more restless as the hurricane's effects began.

By the time Jenna had called me to see about joining them to volunteer at the school, I was all volunteered out. Plus, I knew Bett wouldn't let me go off the property at that point.

By six, I went up to the house and put a frozen lasagna in the oven, knowing it would take forever to cook. I knew no one else would think of food, and with me, Bett, my uncle Jack, and possibly a few other volunteers still around the place, people would be hungry soon enough. We also had frozen garlic bread and the makings of a salad from the garden, so I washed the lettuce and got that stuff ready too. Then I made a small pile of apples and carrots to bring down to the horses for a treat later.

Sighing heavily, I sat down at the kitchen table and looked around. All was silent except the tick of the clock that sat on the mantel in the living room. Bett's house was small—the rooms were snug, and the ceilings were low. I guess you could say it was cozy. It got a lot of light on sunny days, and there were rag rugs on the worn wooden floors, and around the fireplace were two big sofas and two cushy chairs that swallowed you up when you sat in them.

There were three tiny bedrooms—mine (which was my dad's childhood room), Bett's, and a guest room that Uncle Jack used when he came—plus a small living room, a kitchen with an eating area, and two bathrooms. The laundry was in the basement, and that was all. The place wasn't dirty, but everything was beat-up and there were piles of stuff all around—clean laundry I'd folded, but hadn't yet put away, clean dishes I'd left in the dish drainer and hadn't had time to put away, stacks of Bett's paperwork, old newspapers to recycle, a diorama of the solar system I was working on for school, stuff like that. I guess you could say it was lived-in—cozy and cheerful—but it was small and cluttered. That's what happens when the same family lives somewhere for, like, a hundred years. Junk just becomes part of the scenery.

The Petries' house was the opposite of ours: Everything in it had beauty and was in perfect condition. The place was immaculately clean, and there weren't any piles of unfinished work or clutter—the housekeepers made sure of that—and the spacious, high-ceilinged rooms were decorated in pretty colors and fabrics, with tasteful accessories and artwork all around. The houseman did the chores—shopping, cleaning the grill, getting gas in the cars—anything that needed doing. The Petries didn't eat frozen lasagna for dinner—their cook made fresh and delicious meals all day long, with warm cookies in the afternoons and bacon for breakfast every morning. Campbell's bed was made for her, and her laundry was washed and crisply ironed each day. The house had a beautiful freshwater pool and that amazing wraparound porch where you could just sit and relax and watch the boats go by all day long—no one expected you to take care of anything!

It was heaven, and I hoped no harm would come to it during the hurricane.

The rain was starting to come down for real now, and I switched on the TV like I usually do when I'm home alone (which is most of the time, since Bett seems to live at the barn). A lot of the time, I leave it on in the living room even if I'm in my bedroom, because it sounds like people are here, and it makes me feel not so alone.

Now, I turned to the news to see what was happening. The reporter Tabitha Jones came on and then she was showing around inside my school.

"Oh my god!" I jumped up and went closer to the set. "That's my school!" I cried out loud.

But there was no one for me to tell. I watched carefully as they panned around the scene—they had that Bud Slater guy on talking about the evacuation and encouraging people to come down and "use the resources the town is providing." Then they showed all around the gymnasium, and I saw the school nurse and then—*What?!*—it was Jenna and Selena! My jaw dropped as I watched them being interviewed. I couldn't believe it! Then the news showed them singing with the kids and that Tabitha Jones interviewing them, and they looked great.

I was so excited! I kept wanting someone to come in—anyone!—so I could share this with them, but I was all alone. I quickly texted my mom to tell her, then I texted Jenna and Selena that they were amazing on TV and told them to call me when they could. Then the report drifted into the weather update, and I sank back down in my seat, musing about how cool that had been to see my school and my friends on TV.

According to the weatherman, the first part of the hurricane was still thirty miles offshore, but it was due to really hit us within the next two hours. Wind speeds were predicted to be up to one hundred miles per hour by eleven o'clock, and the rain was going to be major—five inches by midnight, they were saying. Combined with the tide and the sizes of the waves, we were in for major flooding.

The lights flickered suddenly, and I groaned.

Oh no, not the power. Not yet! I thought. But then they came right back on.

I went to see if the oven was still going, and luckily it was. With a gas oven, only the pilot light was electric, so at least we'd have hot food even if the power went out.

We've had storms before where the power went out, and I really hate it. You can't charge your phone and there's no TV, and you can only open the fridge for like a second or all the cold escapes. After a while, our hot water runs out, so there are no more hot showers. I wished we had a generator. I was sure the Petries had a generator—they could probably light up their whole house with whichever one they had. They'd never even notice if the power went out!

I decided to take a shower before anything else happened, and then I came back to check on the lasagna. It was pretty close to ready. My mom had texted me back that it was exciting about my friends, and she'd look for the clip online later, then she cautioned me again to be careful in the storm and helpful to Bett.

"Yeah, yeah," I texted her back, but I added a smiley face.

Bett and Jack were on the back porch now, stomping and taking off their boots, and I flew to the door to swing it open for them.

"Thanks, honey. Phew! This one's shaping up to be a doozy!" said Bett.

"Smells great in here! What have you got on?" said Uncle Jack, sniffing the air.

"Lasagna. And salad with garlic bread. Is anyone else coming?"

"No, I sent them all home," said Bett. "People need to

be with their families in storms like this. You never know what could happen."

We were all quiet for a second, thinking of what could happen.

"Are you scared?" I asked.

"I wouldn't say scared, but concerned," said Bett. "I'm going back down to the barn after we eat and rest a spell. The horses are not going to like this one bit, and I'll need to stay with them."

"All night?" I asked, stunned.

"If that's what it takes," shrugged Bett, pouring herself a lemonade.

"I'll do it, Bett," said Uncle Jack. (Even Bett's children call her Bett.)

But Bett shook her head. "You can do what you like, but I'll be staying there."

Dinner was delicious, actually, and after I'd cleaned up and the dishwasher was humming (for now), Bett stood up and stretched. "Piper, you're the best. I don't know what I'd do without you. You keep everything in order, and you've always got the home fires burning. I'm going to take a quick shower to limber up these tired old bones, then I'm heading back down to the barn. Thanks again for dinner, sweetheart." Bett kissed me on the top of my head and went into her room and closed the door.

Uncle Jack was watching the TV, and he turned to look at me kindly. "Piper, it's such a good thing you're here. I'm so grateful to you for looking after Bett."

"Me, looking after her?" I was surprised. "But she's the one who looks after me!" I said.

But Uncle Jack laughed. "I think if you really think about it, you'll see that the opposite is true. You're a wonderful caretaker, and you create such a nice environment everywhere you go. I appreciate it and I know my mom does too. She couldn't do any of this without you. She's not exactly a homemaker. More of a cowboy." He chuckled again.

"Huh," I didn't know what to say, I was so surprised. I'd never thought that *I* was the one looking after *Bett*. I mean, I do the laundry and cooking, and most of the cleaning. I guess I'm the one who makes sure Bett eats and sometimes I tell her to go to bed if she's up late. But it hadn't occurred to me that she wouldn't do this all on her own.

Bett came back from her shower and thanked me again, then she and Uncle Jack went back to the barn.

"Call me on the landline down there if you need us, okay honey? Don't hesitate," said Uncle Jack. "I'll be back in a flash if you call."

The sun was setting somewhere up there in the sky, behind all the rain clouds, and darkness was closing in. Jack had given me a huge flashlight ("just in case"), and I put it on the coffee table, then plugged my phone in to charge and pulled an old heavy quilt over me and settled in to watch the Hallmark Channel on TV, alternating with the weather reports. And sure enough, about forty-five minutes into my show, the house was suddenly plunged into darkness. Total and complete inky darkness, the kind where you keep opening your eyes wider as if that will help you see something. And this time the power didn't come right back on.

I sat in place on the sofa, fumbling for the flashlight and trying to decide if I should just snuggle in and go to sleep right where I was. But it wasn't that late—only nine o'clock—and I wasn't tired. I peered around in the blackness and tried to make out shapes. Outside, the wind howled, and the branch of a hydrangea bush was tapping against the side of the house. Then the tapping grew stronger and became more of a knock. *Wait!* It *was* a knock! Someone was knocking on the back door, and I was all alone! I fumbled for my phone to call down to the barn, and I flicked on the flashlight and shone it around.

Right then the light landed on a face in the big picture window in the kitchen, and I screamed and dropped the phone and the light and pulled the blanket over my head.

CHAPTER 12

Ziggy

FRIDAY NIGHT

After Samantha and I walked the dogs and I chatted again with Mrs. MacNichol at the shelter, Jenna's mom came to pick us up. I hugged Selena tightly and even gave Samantha a little squeeze. She's quiet but she seems pretty nice, I think.

"Stay safe, girls," I said. "Shalom." (I learned this word in Israel this summer—it means "peace" and you can say it as a greeting or a farewell.)

"Shalom aleichem," said Samantha back, surprising me with the more formal version of the goodbye.

"I thought you were British!" I said, blinking in amazement.

Samantha smiled and shrugged. "My dad's Israeli."

Now I was confused. "But...your skin..." I didn't know how to phrase it, but her skin color wasn't that of a native Israeli.

Now she laughed. "My mom's Somalian. I'm a mutt."

"Cool!" I said in admiration. "You're so lucky to have all these cultures!"

She laughed and nodded. "Depends on the day. Depends on which granny is annoying me!"

"Also lucky! I want to hear more but I have to go. Come back soon so we can hang out again!" I said, envying her multiple grandmothers.

Riding back to my house, which isn't too far, Jenna was telling us how she was in shock about some girl from her swim team showing up at the shelter, but Mrs. Bowers interrupted her to ask me about our hurricane preparedness. I had to admit that other than boarding the chickens and having solar power already, we hadn't done anything.

"What about that pond you have out back?" she asked. "Isn't it an estuary?"

"You mean, like, is it connected to the bay?"

She nodded. "Yes. I'm just thinking about tidal surges."

"Oh. Um. Yes?"

"You'd better keep an eye on it. It's awfully close to the back of your house."

"I know. But nothing's ever happened with it before. My mom thinks this whole storm is kind of exaggerated. Anyway, we have solar power and a well, so we are all self-sufficient!"

"So, you can watch TV all night, even if the power's still out?" said Jenna with a teasing grin.

I swatted Jenna. "You know we don't have a TV, silly."

Mrs. Bowers looked at me nervously in the rearview mirror. "How will you follow the storm's progress?"

I shrugged. "We have a little radio in the kitchen. Maybe on that?"

Mrs. Bowers pulled into our driveway. Our lights were shining brightly, and the Prius was in the driveway. The house looked cozy in the gloomy rain.

"Thanks, Mrs. Bowers. And Jenna, that was a good idea, to volunteer. Thanks for asking me. Bye!"

"Ziggy!" called Mrs. Bowers, just as I was about to shut the car door. I turned back. "Sweetheart, we have plenty of food and plenty of room at our house, if you need anything. Please come over, anytime. Honestly. Do you want me to come in and invite your mom in person?"

I hurried to shake my head no. "Thanks so much. I'll tell her." All I needed was for Mrs. Bowers to hear my mom's off-the-wall anti-hurricane theories, and I'd never be invited anywhere with Jenna again!

"I mean it!" Mrs. Bowers called as I closed the door and trotted inside, dodging raindrops.

And thank goodness Mrs. Bowers offered, because it wasn't too long before I began to seriously consider it.

The rain started to become heavy shortly after they dropped me off. My mom was working on one of her quilts in the living room, and my dad was making tomato sauce for the food pantry with the tomatoes he'd set aside. I wasn't sure, but it seemed like my parents were in a fight for some reason.

I hung out in the kitchen at first, watching my dad, listening to the rain pound the metal roof above us, and trying to get my dad to tell me who that lady was today on Brookfield Lane, the one who'd known his name.

"Oh, just someone I know from...town politics," he'd said dismissively.

"Hmm. She seemed upset."

My dad looked up at me and then he shrugged casually. "I think she was worried I'd been hurt."

I watched him for an extra few seconds. Something was weird about him, but I couldn't tell what.

"She seemed...nice," I said, trying to get him to tell me more.

He looked up at me in surprise. "She is. Uh...you'd like her."

But we were interrupted by a loud crack and a crashing sound outside, and my dad and I rushed to the window and cupped our hands over the glass to see what we could see outside. It was then that I noticed the pond.

"Dad! Look at the water!"

The pond was halfway up our back yard.

"Lisa!" called my dad urgently. "Lisa! Come look at this!"

My mom scurried in and looked out the window. "Wow!" she breathed. "When's high tide today?" she asked.

My dad went to look it up in the newspaper and returned with a grim look on his face. "Nine o'clock," he said.

"But it's only seven o'clock now and look how high it is!" said my mom in surprise.

"Right," he agreed. "This isn't good. That water's coming in here."

"What should we do?" asked my mom.

My dad sighed and laid out a plan that we followed for the next two hours.

We don't have a basement because we're so close to the wetlands as it is, so we had to focus on the fact that the water could come into our first floor. We moved everything we could upstairs. The stuff that wouldn't go up, we stacked downstairs, with the upholstered furniture on top of the plain wood furniture, to keep the fabric from getting wet. It was sweaty work and stressful because every time I checked, the water was closer to our back door.

What we really needed were sandbags, to lay at the doors and hopefully keep some of the water from coming in. But we didn't have any and my parents bickered about it.

"We should have been more ready!" my father complained.

"How could I have known this was all for real?" said my mom.

My father sighed in aggravation. "Because dozens of people said so, and the news said so, and the papers said so."

"*You* should have gotten all these supplies if you knew there was such a big storm coming."

"I can't do everything myself!" my dad complained, and so on.

I hate it when my parents fight—there's no one for me to discuss it with or roll my eyes with or be a little scared with. And since there are only three of us, they always want me on their side to break the tie. It's kind of like when your two best friends are in a fight. There's no winning for you!

"Ziggy, don't you agree that..." and "Ziggy, tell your mother..." and I finally threw my hands in the air like a traffic cop and yelled, "Stop!"

Once I had their attention, I continued. "Listen, people. I already told you that Jenna's parents said we could go over there if we wanted. I think we should just get this place in the best shape we can—maybe put some of mommy's quilts at the doors—and then leave before we're underwater. What do you say?"

My mom sighed. "I hate to impose. Can't we just go to the school?" she seemed defeated.

But my dad shook his head. "It's too risky to drive all the way over there. The Bowers' is much closer. I think Ziggy has a point. We should go."

Twenty minutes later, we left our house and dashed to the car. The water was at the back steps and it was only eight thirty; high tide at nine would bring it even higher, probably in through the back door. Even the short run from the house to the Prius left us all soaked. All the way to the Bowerses' my dad drove very cautiously. Above us the wind caused the tree limbs to flail, ripping away their fresh green leaves and churning them through the air like confetti. The rain was coming down so hard you could barely see out the car windows. I knew my dad was thinking of his near-miss earlier, and I winced each time

I heard a crash outside. The town was in total darkness as we drove, which was really spooky—no streetlights, very few lights on in houses, except for the ghostly flicker of candles and the occasional brightly lit room that must've been using a generator. It was kind of like driving through a war zone.

We were all silent in the car, as if by focusing our attention, we could keep ourselves safe all the way to the Bowerses' house. I think we all knew that if one of us opened our mouth, it could only be to say, "We shouldn't be outside or driving right now."

We finally pulled up to the Bowerses', which was in almost total darkness except for the kitchen / family room. There were a ton of cars parked outside, and my mom didn't want to go in at the last minute.

"Get out of the car, Lisa," said my dad firmly. "We're going in." I was happy to hear him taking charge.

My mom was all fluttery and nervous, but my dad strode to the back door, knocked, and in we went.

Inside, the Bowerses were so happy to see us! Besides Jenna, her parents, and her three little brothers, Jenna's grandparents were there and a bunch of her cousins and some aunts and uncles. They had a huge feast laid out on the kitchen counters—all the savory dishes and sweet treats from her family's farm stand, plus big bowls of wild blueberries, piles of tomatoes, and more. I realized that I was starving—we'd never had dinner—and we were quickly given heaping plates of food and settled onto sofas to eat.

I turned to my dad. "This is nice," I said. "Having a big family is so nice."

He nodded. "Yes. It is," he croaked. Then he cleared his throat.

"I wish we had this," I added, looking around at all the happy faces that looked so similar—the Bowers clan.

He nodded again and smiled at me, but he seemed to have tears in his eyes again! What was going on with him?

"I'm so glad mom finally came around," I said, looking

at her chatting happily in the kitchen with Jenna's mom. I was hugely relieved to be out of our house and with other people. It had been scary when it was just the three of us, fighting the storm all alone. But now, in a big group, I felt safe.

Jenna plopped on the floor at my feet. "I hope your house is okay," she said.

"Me too," I agreed. "Thanks for having us!"

"I never thought you'd come. I'm so psyched!"

Jenna's dad called out to my dad. "Josh, let's go back to your place after you've eaten. The eye of the storm will be passing soon, so we'll have a little window of safety to be out there. I've got some sandbags in the garage and we can see if we can rig up a pump too," he said. Jenna's uncles and her grandfather chimed in. "We'll come help."

One of the uncles offered up some skill of his and the others had some funny story about it, which they laughed and teased him for, and soon they were all affectionately ragging on each other and laughing. It was fun, and funny and also cozy. I looked around the room. I thought about our small house with just the three of us in it, and I just wished I had a big family like this.

This is what matters, I thought. *Being with your family and looking out for one another.*

CHAPTER 13

Jenna

EARLY SATURDAY MORNING

It was fun having the Blooms sleep over and all my cousins and everyone. I woke up in a panic after the eye of the storm passed us and the hurricane picked back up again. It was the middle of the night—three o'clock by my watch— and the rain was hitting the roof so forcefully it sounded like someone was throwing buckets of water on the shingles. The wind was roaring again, causing branches to clack against each other and the loose hinges on the garage door made it rattle and bang. Would this never end? I got up to go to the bathroom and get a drink of water, stepping carefully over Ziggy, who was asleep on the beanbag in my room. I was surprised to hear the grown-ups still chatting quietly out in the living room, the low hum of a radio keeping them company. I was glad that my family and the Blooms had come here and not gone to the shelter at school. I mean, the shelter was fine, but this was better.

I thought back to my shock at seeing Franny Barnes and her parents at school earlier. They'd stood in the doorway of the gym in some kind of shock, and since all of the lifeguards were busy settling other arrivals, I'd gone over to them to help.

"Franny?" I'd said.

She'd turned to me with that sort of blank look she wears, and then her eyes had snapped into focus. "Hi, Bowers," she said. I wondered if she thought that was actually my first name.

"I'm volunteering here. Can I help you to some cots?"

"Thank you, dear," agreed Franny's dad. He was clutching two small suitcases.

"Come on, follow me," I said. "What happened with the swim meet?" I asked. My voice was casual, but my heart was thumping. "I thought you went up to Salem yesterday, to get ahead of the storm."

Franny's mom was nodding. "They canceled it—"

"Then we decided to drive home—" said her dad.

"—and our car got smashed by a falling branch—" said her mom.

"—a tree fell on our house," finished Franny.

My hands flew to my mouth in horror. "I'm so sorry!" I said, and I meant it. Those were both horrible things to happen. "Is your house damaged badly?"

"No, but the car is. The tree just pulled down the power lines with it, so we can't stay there until the power company comes and fixes it," said Mr. Barnes.

I nodded. "And your car?"

"The hood is crushed, but it's drivable." He nodded.

"Thank goodness you weren't hurt," I said, and I meant that too.

"It's sad about the meet," said Franny woodenly.

I would have thought she'd be more upset. I just nodded. "Yeah, I agree. Bummer."

We were both quiet for a moment. I was thinking about all my hard work. Franny was probably thinking about beating me.

"Do you need anything?" I offered. "There are donated toiletry kits over here. I can bring you some. Or food? The cafeteria is open for snacks and they're serving dinner in there at six thirty. Anything?"

Mrs. Barnes shook her head. "Thank you. You've been so kind. We have all our things from the trip to Salem right here. Franny gets so unsettled with changes, you know, because of her challenges. That's why we wanted to get her up to Salem and acclimated before race day."

"Her challenges?" I asked.

Her mom looked at me in confusion. "Her autism. It makes transitions and change difficult for her."

Autism? Franny was autistic? My jaw dropped. "Oh, I… I didn't realize. I didn't know…" I stammered. I could feel my face burning with embarrassment. How could I have been so clueless and insensitive?

But Mrs. Barnes was kind. "Really? That makes for a nice change. People can usually tell pretty quickly, and they treat her differently than they treat other kids. But not you—you've always been so friendly."

I blinked, still shocked. "I couldn't tell. Not at all, actually."

"Funny. It's such a part of Franny's life that I always assume all of her friends know." Mrs. Barnes watched Franny, who was now sitting on the edge of a cot while her dad talked quietly to her. "Anyway, you're so nice to help us. Thank you so much. It means a lot. We didn't come here lightly. It's so disruptive for her. But we were really scared to stay in the house."

"Please, if there's anything I can do..." I offered. My brain was whirling, trying to process this information.

Mrs. Barnes smiled and shook her head. "You already have. It's wonderful for Franny to see a friend here. It's just what she needs to help put her at ease. Thank you." She beamed at me and shook my hand, then she pulled me in for a hug. "Thank you for helping us."

"My pleasure," I said as she released me. "Let me just go say bye to Franny."

I sat on the bed opposite Franny and her dad. She was serious, as always, but I had a new sensitivity to it now. I spoke quietly. "Franny, tonight will be nice. There are good people here and good food. Everyone will be here to look after you guys. Maybe you'd like to say hi to some of the dogs once you're settled in." I looked at her dad for confirmation.

He smiled and nodded. "Franny loves dogs," he said.

"Dogs," agreed Franny.

I patted her on her knee. "Everything will be okay," I said.

It's really, really weird to suddenly have compassion for someone you've (I had to admit it) disliked for a long time. It's really weird to learn something like this about someone you thought you knew. I mean, we don't have much of a chance to talk in swim practice or at meets. I just always thought Franny was cold and a snob; that she was focused, driven, competitive. But knowing that she had autism now made me understand her difficulty in social situations. The fact that her mom had twice called me Franny's friend made me want to get to know her better. She was still my most worthy competitor, but I was no longer offended by her behavior.

Working at the shelter yesterday, singing with the kids, settling in the Barneses, and then hosting the Blooms—it had taken my mind off the meet and my own problems. It had made me feel good. It had made other people feel good.

This is what matters, I thought as I climbed the ladder back up to my loft bed. *Helping others.*

CHAPTER 14

Selena

EARLY SATURDAY MORNING

My papí came by late last night during the eye of the storm.
The Frankels' house had held fast so far—no damage, no
flooding. It was set high on a dune, gracias a Díos, so even
though the water came close, it could not get in. That the
Frankels had spent a fortune on dune management—
putting in fiber blankets and cables under the sand and
planting in zillions of baby beach grasses—was probably

what saved the dune from crumbling away and taking the house with it.

I was so grateful for my papí's quick visit and the update. I squeezed him tightly before he left and gave him a big kiss.

"Be careful, papíto," I whispered.

"I will, tesoro," he agreed.

I woke up very early Saturday morning, blinking at my unfamiliar surroundings, then realizing where I was. People were rustling all around me, getting up and wandering to the bathrooms. I wanted to look out the window.

In the hall outside the gym were big plateglass windows that looked out to the lawn and the sidewalk and road beyond. There were a zillion leaves on the ground, and one tree was down across the street, just like the one that had nearly nailed us in the cafeteria last night. The day was cloudy, but it wasn't raining any longer, and I could see some blue sky on the horizon. I went back into the gym.

"Mamí," I said, gently poking her.

She sat bolt upright and blinked.

"It's okay," I said, giggling. "We're in the shelter, at my school."

"Ay," she said, lying back down on the cot, but with her eyes open.

"Mamí , how do you think our house is?"

"I'm sure everything is fine. Your papí will probably come soon to get us. We should get ready." She sat up and swung her legs over the edge of the cot and stuffed them into her Toms shoes.

People were beginning to shuffle around, and as they passed, they greeted us.

Mrs. Waters said, "Selena! I'm so happy we got to spend some time together and that I got to hear your wonderful singing voice. I'm looking forward to working with you on the musical!"

Bud Slater came through and said, "Thank you for helping with the children yesterday. You made a big difference to them. It was generous of you. You should think about joining the Junior Lifeguard program next summer."

Samantha Frankel heard all the chatter and woke up. "Thanks for including me, Selena," she said. "It was fun volunteering here. And those lifeguards were really cool."

After Samantha left for the bathroom, my mamí sat on my cot and wrapped me in her arms. "Selena, mi amor. You are so wonderful. People love you. You are generous and kind and talented."

"Thanks, mamí," I said. "Too bad I'm looking so ugly on the outside!" I joked.

My mom pulled back and studied my face. "Actually, it is almost all gone. And you are never ugly on the outside, especially not to me. But you know what? You have enough going for you on the inside. Si?" she said. She stood up and patted me on the head and walked off to the ladies' room.

Sitting all alone, looking around my school gym at all the brave hurricane survivors, I realized no one cared how they looked. We were all lucky to be alive, lucky to be together, lucky to have been kind and supportive to each other, cooperating under bad circumstances. How any of us looked had nothing to do with it.

This is what matters, I thought. *What's inside.*

CHAPTER 15

Piper

SATURDAY MORNING

I almost died of fright last night. The blackout, the knock-
ing, the face in the window—OMG! But then I heard voices
calling, "Piper! Bett? Anyone?"

I dashed to the door and flung it open, the wind practically tearing it from my hand, and there were the Petries—
Campbell and her parents. They fell into the house and
nearly collapsed on the kitchen floor, drenched with rain.

"What happened?" I'd asked. "Here, give me your jackets."

I put the big flashlight face up in the middle of the kitchen table, so it cast a wide pool of light on the ceiling that reflected all around. While I hung their dripping rain clothes on hooks by the door, I listened to their tale.

"Water came way up—" her dad blurted.

"Porch ripped off and washed away—" added her mom.

"We thought the whole house was going out to sea!" cried Campbell. "It was awful, Piper. We fled!"

"I've got to borrow your phone, please," said Mr. Petrie.

"I can't believe it," I said. "I just can't believe it. Let me call down to the barn. Let's see if we can help!" I dialed the barn phone, and Uncle Jack picked up right away. I explained that the Petries were here, and he said he'd be right up.

I sat with Campbell at the table while her parents stood at the phone, calling the police, fire department, everyone. There was nothing anyone could do for now. The only good thing was they'd turned off their gas line earlier so there was no gas flowing into the house that could blow everything up.

Campbell was crying softly. "Piper, it was so scary."

I reached out for her hand, and she grabbed mine with a death grip and held on tightly, while the storm raged relentlessly outside.

I pictured that gorgeous house, that porch I was on just yesterday, how close the ocean was, how low-lying the house. I closed my eyes and shuddered. They could have died!

Then Uncle Jack and Bett were there, bustling around, making tea, offering food, taking charge. They sent me and Campbell into my room and set up the Petries with clean towels and assigned them the room Jack usually stays in (he'd be sleeping on the living room sofa, *no ifs ands or buts about it*, he'd said.) The adults gathered in the kitchen and their voices rose and fell. Campbell and I got ready for bed and we each climbed into one of the pair of twin beds in my room.

Campbell yawned. "I'll never be able to fall asleep!" she said.

We spoke for a few moments, with Campbell telling me how relieved she was to be staying in my house.

"Our house is scary," she said to me. "I know it sounds spoiled, but it's too big. Everyone's so far away, and it's a hassle if you forget something way up on the third-floor playroom and then you have to go get it. And there are always a lot of people working there, so there's no privacy, and you have to be nice all the time. You can't fight with your siblings or your parents, and it's all like you're acting in a play. The happy family play. The place is like a museum, everything is fragile or expensive. You can't be anywhere in a wet bathing suit—" Campbell yawned grandly. "I know I sound horrible and spoiled. I just like being in a normal house like this. Happy and snug, with everyone right here and no fakeness, no phony baloney. Just real." She yawned again loudly then went silent.

"Yeah..." I agreed, but I was still processing everything

she'd said. Was it really like that at their house? Phony and uncomfortable and inconvenient? It was hard to see it that way at first, but as I imagined actually living there, I began to see what she meant. But would she give it up? For real, for something like this?

"Cam?" I whispered into the darkness.

But she was out like a light.

I actually couldn't fall asleep with all the excitement of the day and now the bad news about the Petries' house. I prayed it would survive.

Bett came in to check on me right after Campbell fell asleep. "Okay, Pipe?" she whispered, sitting down on the edge of my bed and stroking my hair like I was a horse. She used to do that when I was younger, but it had been a while.

"How are the horses?" I asked. I felt so close to them that it agonized me to think of them scared and possibly suffering.

Bett smiled. "They're tough, our horses. They're going

to be fine. Layla had a bit of an upset when the barn doors blew open at one point, but she's unscathed. I've got to get back down there, though. I can't leave them, the poor creatures. They have no idea what's going on. They must think it's the end of the world."

I nodded. I understood how she felt. The horses trusted us and relied on us to look after them.

Bett continued. "Thanks again for all of your help today, sweetheart. You are such a star. You're the rock of the family, always keeping things running, looking after us all," she whispered. "I love you."

"Love you too, Bett," I said as she bent to kiss my forehead.

"Sleep well, sweetheart."

"You too."

"I'll be at the barn if you need me. Just call. Jack will be here."

My phone brightened in the dark just after she left. It was a text from my mom.

Love you, sweet pea. Thanks for looking after Bett. So glad you are safe. Xoxo Mom

As I drifted off to sleep, I knew I had the topic for my paper.

This is what matters. Not money, not fancy houses with maids and gardeners, swimming pools and catered meals, but safety. Plain old, cozy safety.

CHAPTER 16

Ziggy

LATE SATURDAY MORNING

There were so many people in Jenna's house when I finally woke up this morning, I couldn't believe it! I'd tried to do a little wake-up yoga in Jenna's room—my back was like a pretzel after sleeping on the beanbag—but there wasn't the floor space I needed, and I couldn't really do it in the living room because there were so many people there.

The kitchen was filled with Bowers relatives who

hadn't even spent the night. They'd just shown up this morning with more food and supplies (things like a coffee maker that worked on the gas stove top, because there was no electricity to run the usual one). People were talking a mile a minute, and loudly! It was chaotic. I had to go outside to get a little centered.

On the back porch, I found my mom.

"Hi Ziggy Stardust," she said, a big mug of tea in her hand. She patted the wooden plank next to her, and I sat and snuggled against her as she wrapped her arm around me tightly.

"It's so noisy in there," I whispered.

"And crowded," she agreed.

We giggled. Then she said, "Ziggy, I need to apologize to you for being irresponsible. I let my politics get in the way of my common sense, and by refusing to prepare for the hurricane, I put you in danger and it scared the heck out of me. I feel terrible. I'm so sorry." She squeezed me to her side.

"It's okay, mommy," I said. She likes it when I call her that, so I throw her a few "mommys" now and then.

She sighed. "I hope our house isn't too waterlogged. Poor Dad and the Bowers were there until all hours. But one of Jenna's uncles rigged a great pump system with our garden hose, believe it or not, and he was able to pump out the water that came in."

"Was there a lot?" I asked, sitting bolt upright.

She nodded. "At first. There was about six inches. But they got it out and got it under control. It didn't sit for long in the house, but we have some work to do. Thank goodness you made us come here. Who knows what we would have done all alone in that house, with the water rising?"

I nodded. "It's nice to have a big family. People who can help you."

My mom nodded. "Mm-hmm," she said thoughtfully.

"I wish we had that," I added. "I mean, maybe not all the time."

She smiled at me. "It's a little noisy, having a big family, right?"

I giggled. "Yes. A small family is just right. Want to go home?"

She nodded. "Yes. Let's go find dad and head out. This was fun, and I'm so grateful to all the Bowerses, but I need some alone time. Even if it has to be upstairs."

"Me too!" I agreed.

After we said our goodbyes and thank-yous and hopped in the old Prius, I thought about the hurricane and the sleepover at Jenna's with all of her relatives. It had been fun, but I was happy to have my parents back to myself, and I was looking forward to the peace and quiet of our house, even if the floor downstairs was a little dampish.

This is what matters, I thought. *Loving the family you have.*

CHAPTER 17

Jenna

SATURDAY AFTERNOON

My friends and I had made a plan to meet at the Lookout
Beach parking lot at three o'clock, and we all arrived right
at the same time, on bikes: me, Selena, Piper, Ziggy, and
Samantha. We looked at one another and smiled. We'd made
it. The hurricane had been scary and tiring, hard and damaging, but we'd all come through, as had most of the Cape.
There'd been lots of storm damage—the worst I'd heard

was that Piper's friends the Petries had lost their porch and their pool house—and people all along the coast had flooding damage, trees down, and power out, but there'd been no deaths and no miles-long traffic jams, or anything.

Biking to meet my friends, it was hard to believe the change in the weather. From the wild wind and humidity of yesterday's storm to today's cool and breezy air, and not a cloud in the sky, all in just twenty-four hours. But the storm's damage was everywhere. I saw people all over town working industriously to clean up and repair the aftermath. I cycled around a huge wood chipper hitched to the back of a town garbage truck on Ocean Avenue. It was inching its way along, as two sanitation workers fed enormous fallen tree branches into its hungry, noisy mouth. There were families in their yards raking leaves—it was funny to see huge raked piles of green leaves, rather than the usual red, gold, and orange that we get in the fall—and up on ladders clearing their rain gutters. I saw two men hoisting a fallen shutter and working to rehang it on their house.

Some stores in town had shattered windows despite the tape they'd put up, and there were random bits of scattered trash everywhere—loose bricks, a sneaker, plastic water bottles, a boogie board. The town looked terrible, but there was joy in the air. We'd been lucky on the Cape this time.

As my friends and I shared our storm stories, we realized we'd all learned important things about ourselves and our priorities, and we laughed when we realized we each had our thesis ready for our "What Matters" English essay. Samantha seemed thrilled by the whole hurricane experience, declaring it "wicked good fun," her "favorite storm ever," and "so much better than boarding school." But she was relieved to not have to write an essay about it, citing her dyslexia and other learning differences.

"If I had to, I'd write about sleeping in the shelter," she said. "I've never stayed with strangers like that before, and I've certainly never slept in a gymnasium. I guess what matters to me are ironed sheets and an immaculate bathroom!"

I was pretty sure that Samantha was joking, but I could feel the rest of us cringing as we silently acknowledged that it was the work of Mrs. Diaz that gave Samantha "what mattered." She wasn't one of us, that much was for sure. I doubted we'd ever see her again, so it wasn't worth calling her out on her insensitivity.

"Wow! The beach got chowed!" I said instead, changing the subject as we reached the bike rack at the top of the hill. I saw Selena shoot me a grateful smile, and I nodded once in return.

Lookout Beach was about half its usual size.

Piper nodded. "We're lucky it wasn't worse. The beach could come back over the winter, though. It depends on the tides and what other kinds of storms we have. Some storms deposit sand and others take them away."

"Gosh, it looks so weird!" I said. "It's like someone ate half of it." There looked to be a steep drop-off where the water met the sand. I wanted to investigate.

"How about your friend's house, Piper?" asked Ziggy

with wide eyes. "We only had flood damage at my house, and that was bad enough. I can't believe they lost a whole section of their home!"

Piper looked crestfallen. "I love that house. I would have been a wreck if the whole thing had washed away. The Petries are going to rebuild it and they're planning to work with the Nature Conservancy and a program at UMass to try some experimental solutions for creating a series of dunes in front." Suddenly, she brightened. "Wow! Look at all those lifeguards!"

About twenty-five or thirty kids in red lifeguard T-shirts had just swarmed off the deck of the beach pavilion, and were now deploying all around the beach, raking sand, dragging debris up to the garbage area, putting the lifeguard stand back up, raising the *No Swimming* flag, and more. They reminded me of marines, landing on a foreign battleground and getting things ready for the invading forces. My chest swelled with admiration. Lifeguarding was looking pretty cool to me these days.

Bud Slater was there, bossing them all around like a general, but he turned and caught sight of us.

"What are you waiting for?" he called in his booming voice as he waved us down to help. "We need you!"

This is also what matters, I thought, deep in my heart. *Being a lifeguard.*

DON'T MISS THE NEXT
SUMMER LIFEGUARDS
ADVENTURE!

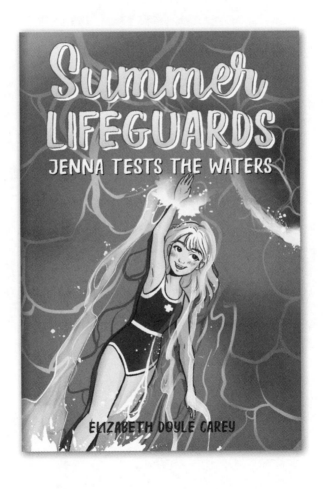

A Bright Idea

All I ever wanted was to be an Olympic swimmer. Glory, honor, excellence, patriotism—it all appealed to me. I always pictured myself up there on the top step of the podium in my Ralph Lauren–designed team warm-up suit—red, white, and blue, of course—waving at the crowd, bowing my head for the gold medal, receiving my flowers, and wiping away a modest tear as *The Star-Spangled Banner* played over the sound system for all to hear. The crowd is cheering for me: responsible, reliable, hardworking Jenna

Bowers, from Westham, Massachusetts, as I win the world's highest athletic honor.

More than anything, more even than winning, I love to swim—the relaxation of the pace and rhythm, the feeling of power as I slice through the water. It's hypnotizing and it takes me outside myself for a while, and then it brings me back to earth with a post-workout euphoria. It's what I'm good at, and that skill defines me.

But over the years, my joy in swimming has been replaced by times and stats and schedules, endless meets and practices, unglamorous travel and early mornings, jockeying for position on my own team, and monitoring my standing in my league. If this is all there is, then my Olympic dreams are wavering.

I swim at the Y here in Westham on Cape Cod, where I've been on the team for the past five years. I'd like to say I'm the star of the team, because I was for a really long time. But about six months ago, some new girls joined up, and either they were better or I got worse, and now I'm number three or maybe two on a really good day.

At first, this stunk. I hated being seeded third and watching my coach fall all over these two girls the way she'd once fallen all over me. (I think once my coach realized she wasn't going to be an Olympic swimmer herself, she decided the next best thing would be to "discover" and coach an Olympic swimmer.) It had been fun being the star. But then it started to bother me that when I'd lose, which was rare, everyone would want to pick apart why I'd lost: my coach, my teammates, my parents, and even my brothers! They'd say my breathing was off or my flip turn was too open or I'd been slow off the block. I wanted to say to them all: "Fine! Then you get in the pool, and let's see how you do it!"

And when I started losing more (not badly, by the way—just not winning all the time, like usual), there was more criticism and more hard training, and right then the new girls showed up and, well...after a while, it was kind of fun watching someone else get ripped to shreds after a bad race, and seeing someone else do twenty extra laps for a change. The heat was off, and I felt a lot cooler.

Right about then, maybe a month ago, I saw the first flyer.

It said: "Be a hero! Learn to save lives! Westham Junior Lifeguards tryout info coming soon!" and it gave the website for the town lifeguarding program so you could learn more.

But, most importantly, it was being tacked up on the bulletin board at the YMCA by a really cute high school guy named Luke Slater (not that I actually knew him; I just knew who he was). Physically, he wasn't my type. He was kind of short, and I am tall. He was a little too old for me, and he had white blond hair, while I like guys with dark hair, but his big green eyes were friendly as he called out, "Come on out for tryouts! We're going to post the official date in the next couple of weeks, okay?" And then he grinned at me, so I had to smile back.

"Okay!" I replied, because what else could I say?

I'd heard about kids at school who trained to be Junior Lifeguards; they were always kids I admired but didn't really have time to hang out with because of swimming. When I was younger, we had a babysitter named Molly who did the training every summer and then became an ocean guard. She was so nice and pretty and cool, and on the rare summer weekends when I didn't have a swim meet, I'd head to Lookout Beach for an afternoon where I'd see her at work. She'd sit up high on the lifeguard stand in her red Speedo one-piece and tight ponytail, a whistle around her neck and zinc on her nose. It was like she was the boss of the beach. She'd tell kids what they were and weren't allowed to do and blow her whistle and everyone would obey her. But she'd always wave at me and ask about swim team and how my brothers were. It was like being friends with a celebrity; I was psyched when people would see her talking to me from way up high on her lifeguard throne.

At the end of her shift, the boy lifeguards would often tease her and throw her in the water—everyone would laugh and yell. It looked like so much fun! Like a movie of what being a teenager should be like. Handsome boys joking around with pretty girls in the sunshine at the water's edge, and getting paid for it too! I hadn't seen her much since she'd left for college three years ago, but whenever I thought of lifeguards, I thought of Molly Cruise.

For a while, I'd forgotten about Junior Lifeguards. Then today, a Monday, everything changed. Today's swim practice at the Y started off like any other: I biked over from school, changed into my suit in the locker room, stashed my stuff, and grabbed my goggles and towel. But on my way out to the pool room, I saw a new flyer—a big poster, really.

JUNIOR LIFEGUARD **TRYOUTS** THIS SATURDAY!

10:00 a.m. at the Westham YMCA pool.

Visit our website for forms and details at www.juniorguards.com.

Daily practices M–F 1:00–5:00 p.m. Weekend tournaments.

I felt a little butterfly in my stomach flutter around, but I pushed it away. I had a swim meet up the Cape this weekend, so there was no way I could attend the tryout. Too bad.

In the pool room that day, we had our team meeting on the bleachers, then everyone warmed up and jumped in the water. We worked on our weakest stroke first, and I couldn't stop thinking of the lifeguard tryout as I did the breaststroke up and down the pool. I wondered whether the test would be on certain strokes, or if it would be more about endurance. I'm in really good shape (not to brag), so I knew I could ace an endurance test. If I had to pick a stroke, I'd probably pick butterfly. I bet that would stand out, since most people can't do it.

"Let's go, Bowers! Head out of the clouds, please!" Coach Randall called as she strolled past my lane. How could she tell what I was thinking? I tried harder for a few laps, my head empty of everything but the rhythm: pull, pull, kick, breathe; pull, pull, kick, breathe; pull, pull, kick, breathe. I usually sing a song in my head to keep my rhythm going, but today I had been distracted, so there was no musical accompaniment. Quickly, I started singing the newest Taylor Swift song in my head, and it got me back on track. But then, during a water break, I heard two of the new girls discussing the lifeguard tryouts poster, and I got all distracted again.

"It would be hilarious to watch all those kids splashing around in here, wouldn't it?" said one of them.

The other laughed. "I've heard a couple have to be saved themselves every year!"

"Amateurs!" the first girl laughed.

They were nice girls, but smug and overly secure in their little swim-team world. For some reason, it rubbed me the wrong way today. I thought of Molly and those handsome boy lifeguards. There was nothing amateur about them. If anything, they seemed like professionals, almost adults, to me. Being a lifeguard took nerve! If someone was in trouble in the water, you had to go in and save them, no matter what! Bad weather, sharks, huge waves...anything! It was hard core, like the marines.

Practice was almost over, and it was time for a final time trial, all in, best strokes all around.

Bweeet!

Coach Randall blew her whistle and we were off! I dove in with hardly a splash, then cut through the water and porpoised as far as I could before surfacing for a stroke and a breath. As I said, butterfly is my best stroke, and I've been working for months to shave a few seconds off my time. Every second counted these days.

My wet hand slapped the concrete end of the pool and Coach Randall was there, as always. She clicked her stopwatch and nodded. "Thirty-two seconds. Not your best, Bowers," and then she moved down the lanes. I could see that the two other girls in my heat had beaten me—the ones who'd been talking about the Junior Lifeguard tryouts.

I sighed heavily and snapped my goggles off my eyes so I could massage the dents they'd left in my skin. Slowly, I hoisted myself up and out to change. As I walked to the locker room, I passed the tryouts poster again and felt the butterflies, though this time, there were more of them.

After I showered, changed, pinned up my shoulder-length hair (which used to be blond but is currently light greenish from chlorine), dropped some eye drops into my dark brown eyes, and put on my hoodie, flip-flops, and a layer of bubblegum lip gloss, I slammed my locker shut, grabbed my backpack, and went to unlock my bike and ride home. But just as I cut across the lobby of the Y, I heard Coach Randall calling me from her office.

I turned and saw her at her desk, waving me in. "Hey, Coach," I called. I suddenly felt nervous, but I wasn't sure why.

"Jenna, come on in and take a seat."

Uh-oh, I thought. Coach Randall never calls me by my first name.

"Is something wrong?" I asked, lowering myself onto the chair next to the desk in her cramped office. My mouth was dry, and my heart was thudding. Could she know that I had been fantasizing about Junior Lifeguards?

Coach Randall looked at me kindly. "You seemed a little distracted in there today. Are you okay?" she asked.

Her kindness caught me off guard. We don't really talk about feelings on swim team.

"Oh... I..." I could feel a blush blooming on my cheeks.

"I know things have gotten more competitive around here, but you've always been my star! I just haven't seen your usual effort lately. We have a lot of big meets coming up, and I just wanted to make sure your heart is in it and that nothing's bothering you, on swim team or otherwise." She studied me with her head tipped to the side.

I sighed. It was weird, but it was like something inside me just broke open. I felt my eyes welling up with tears. Coach Randall reached out and put her hand on mine.

"Oh, Jenna! I'm sorry! I didn't mean to make you cry!" With her other hand, she reached for some tissues and handed it to me as I snuffled awkwardly.

"Thanks. I was thinking... It's not about swim team. I do enjoy swim team. I just I thought it might be fun to... I don't know. This is going to sound really bad..."

"Go ahead. It's okay," encouraged Coach Randall.

I took a deep breath and dashed the tears from my eyes. I smiled shakily. "I thought it would be fun to try out for Junior Lifeguards. Absurd, I know! I really don't

232

have time for that. It was just a thought. I'm over it already."

Coach Randall smiled gently and sat back in her seat, folding her arms across her chest. "Is this a sudden thought or something that's been on your mind for a while?"

I sighed. "Ever since I saw the first poster. I guess a few weeks. It just looked like fun, you know?"

Coach Randall sighed too. "I know. It is fun. I did it when I was your age."

"Really?" I asked. I was surprised. It was hard to picture Coach Randall on the beach.

She nodded and swiveled her chair, looking up at the ceiling thoughtfully. "You know, I think a lot about how hard we push you kids these days. Things have become so professional, so competitive. You don't have any free time like we used to when I was your age. It's always on to the next meet, or practice, or test."

I nodded. "I'm used to it, though. I can handle it." I sat up straight. *Brilliant, Bowers*, I scolded myself. *Crying in*

front of your coach about how swim team is no fun! That's a
great way to keep a top spot on the team.

Coach Randall leaned forward again and looked at me carefully. "How about if we make a deal?" she said, squinting.

"What?" I could just imagine where this was heading: extra practices, weight training, more meets...

"How would you like to take the summer off and train with the Junior Lifeguards instead of the swim team? I'll save your spot for you, and you can join back up in the fall. What would you think about that?" She folded her arms again and watched me.

I couldn't help it. A huge smile bloomed on my face. "Wait, *really*? Are you joking?" I looked around the room. "Am I being punked? Is this a trick?"

Coach Randall laughed. "No. It's not a trick. Think of it as cross-training. I think it might renew your interest in swim team if you can get out in the world and see how good your skills are compared to everyone else's. I had the chance to do it when I was a kid, so why shouldn't you?"

"But losing three months of training...and competition. I'll fall so far behind!"

"Tell you what. You can come to practice whenever you like, but we'll say at least once a week. That way you can keep a hand in, and you won't fall out of touch with what's going on. I see your interest level wobbling a bit, and I'd hate to lose you from the team. You've got a ton of talent, and both of us have put a lot of work into your skill development, not to mention your parents and all their time and energy. It would be a shame for all of us if you quit, and it would be a waste for you to stay here when your heart's not in it. If you go on a break starting today, I'll just bet you that you'll come back refreshed and raring to go in September. What do you say?"

COLLECT ALL THE
SUMMER LIFEGUARDS BOOKS!

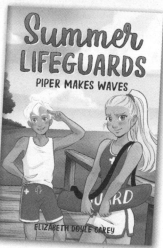

About the Author

Elizabeth Doyle Carey is the author of more than forty books for teens and tweens. A lifelong ocean swimmer, she is scared of big waves and sharks but loves beach glass, dolphins, and whales. Please visit her website at elizabethdoylecarey.com.